Penguin Books
The Sand Dollar

George Sims was born in London in 1923, and was
educated at the Lower School of John Lyon, Harrow. He
served for five years in a Special Communications Unit in
the Army, and then became a dealer in rare books and
manuscripts. He enjoys travelling, particularly in the
Mediterranean and the West Indies, where he can practise
his hobby of underwater swimming. He likes driving fast
cars and is also interested in the cinema. His previous
novels, *The Terrible Door* (1964) *Sleep No More*
(1966), and *The Last Best Friend* (1967), are available in
Penguins. George Sims and his wife Beryl have three
children. They live in Berkshire.

George Sims

The Sand Dollar

Penguin Books

Penguin Books Ltd, Harmondsworth,
Middlesex, England
Penguin Books Australia Ltd, Ringwood,
Victoria, Australia

First published by Victor Gollancz 1969
Published in Penguin Books 1972

Made and printed in Great Britain by
Richard Clay (The Chaucer Press) Ltd
Bungay, Suffolk
Set in Linotype Plantin

To Sheelagh

'Bruised to the breast of Pan, half-god half-brute,
Raked by his bristly boar-sward while he lapped
—Never say kissed her! that were to pollute
Love's language . . .'

ROBERT BROWNING

1

No way out. Nicholas Howard smiled wryly. He was coming to view life more and more as a cul-de-sac, but the sign barring the entrance to Ryder Street had a particular significance for him. He looked past it half expecting to see a parked police car but there was only a night-watchman's hut, a large barrow, and some red lamps marking off the excavated road. On his way to deliver a valuable erotic book to the mysterious Mr Abacus who was known to him only by a brief phone call, his feelings of nervousness and suspicion had been sharpened by the notice. It was a curious situation and he could already visualize himself appearing in court. He said in a hoarse voice that did not sound like his own 'I only wanted to make a crust' and then could hear it being repeated in a policeman's humourless monotone: 'When cautioned the prisoner said "I only wanted to make a crust." '

The biting wind, carrying just a sprinkling of snow, was freezing his face into a stiff mask. He stepped into a doorway, held the parcel between his knees, clapped his hands, then rubbed his face and gingerly felt his painful ears. He listened intently for a moment but no one else seemed to be about in the sepia gloom of this mid-winter evening. He thought : I feel like an imminent accident. His stomach rumbled loudly – he had eaten nothing all day and emptiness was contributing with the bitter cold to induce this pusillanimity.

Suddenly his mood changed. 'To hell with it.' He said this aloud with a bitterness out of proportion to the risk of his furtive errand : it was comment on things in general, proclaiming an indifference to what might be round the corner. Mentally he was always viewing the same landscape, a dreary one of dwindling perspective and rapidly narrowing streets; perpetually re-examining his own sterile ego. Anything unusual would be welcome.

He walked on briskly. It should be interesting to meet Mr Abacus who was not listed in the telephone directory but had one of the most imposing addresses in London. Besides there was little real need to feel guilty about the book with erotic drawings by George Morland – the police should be more interested in the plain pornography that was peddled round Leicester Square. He half-formulated a phrase about eighteenth-century sexual *mores* and then remembered something he had read, how in 1781 George Morland 'had begun to paint *galanteries* for a Drury Lane publisher, to evade all restraint, to drive a phaeton and associate with the demi-monde, and moreover to drink spirits and wine to an extent remarkable even in the late eighteenth century'. Perhaps Morland too had found himself to be in a cul-de-sac.

'Just deliver the book and collect the cheque.' He delivered this self-admonition aloud: talking to himself was becoming a habit; it was living alone that did it.

The illusion that he was walking through a deserted city was dispelled as soon as he set foot in St James's Square. A taxi disappeared round the corner in the direction of Charles Street and he could hear muffled voices on the other side of the square. The sky was clearing rapidly and there was only a handful of high fast-moving clouds; the snow was freezing and resisted his footsteps, sticking to his shoes so that it felt as if he was walking on high heels. He picked a path carefully half-way across Pall Mall but then had to run and jump for the treacherous pavement to escape a rapidly accelerating Volkswagen. He slipped and spun round to regard ruefully the back of the speeding car, thinking how ludicrous it would have been to die there in the frozen slush, clutching a sumptuously bound volume of erotica. Fast on this thought came another that was painful, unbearable, and he blotted it out by wrenching his mind away from its melancholy wanderings to the rapidly approaching confrontation with Mr Abacus. Difficult to visualize him from their telephone conversation. Abacus's voice was light, boyish, and yet he had spoken with unusual authority: the tone had been of someone used to having his instructions carried out immediately.

Brooke House, Carlton Gardens, s.w.i., was easily found. A massive, featureless building, it did not look like a private residence but the headquarters of a merchant bank, constructed from granite to resist an insurrection. Howard's eye was taken by an unusual, sable-coloured car parked outside. It was a miniature Rolls-Royce: it had the current Silver Shadow silhouette, but the chassis was scaled down to about two-thirds size as if it had been built to satisfy the whim of a millionaire child. He glanced in through the side window, noticing that the driver's black hide seat and the controls were specially positioned for a child's convenience.

Suddenly Howard had the feeling that he too was being closely observed, but all the windows of Brooke House were curtained and there was no movement to disclose a watcher. He mounted the wide, shallow steps to the front door and lifted an outsize knocker in the form of intertwined dolphins, beautifully modelled and satisfying to handle. This was it! If one were greedy enough to be willing to act as a pander for a rich man with arcane tastes one must be prepared for any turn of consequences. And, just in case, what was that tongue-twisting phrase, Oscar Wilde's last words before he ignominiously disappeared from the view of the court, bustled below by warders: 'And I, my lord, may I say nothing?'

The door was opened quickly as if his knock had been expected, but swung back only a little way, and then a thin face appeared round the edge to stare blankly at Howard. It was a tall man with tired, watering eyes; he nodded and said 'Er, good evening, sir' so that it contained a hint of a question.

'My name's Howard. A – the bookseller – from New Cavendish Street.' The thin man's face remained expressionless. 'Mr Abacus phoned me – I've got a parcel for him. He's expecting me at seven.' Howard glanced down at his watch as if seeing he was on time would cut through any more hesitation by the guardian of Brooke House. He was only two minutes late.

'H'indeed, sir. A parcel for Mr Abacus. I see, sir. And your name again, sair?' His manner was courteous to the point of seeming like ironic deference; he made no move to open the door wider.

Howard handed in his card and the tall man read it very

slowly as if it was in a foreign language. 'Yes, I see, sir. Mr Nickel-ass Howard.' Somewhere behind him a deep masculine voice said impatiently: 'Show him in, Bishop.'

The hall was luxuriously carpeted but the lighting was so discreet that the first impression of Brooke House was faintly gloomy. The decor was ponderous and there was the sepulchral atmosphere of being in a museum. Howard noticed a silver snipe in a high plaster relief on the ceiling and the wall leading to the staircase on the right was dominated by a very large eighteenth-century oil of a stately woman leaning on a pillar, framed by a lowering sky. Muted sounds of voices, laughter, and music came from somewhere upstairs. Bishop walked ahead slowly as if his feet hurt, showing Howard into a ground floor room that could have housed two squash-courts. Howard sat down in a three-cornered Chinese Chippendale library chair by a marble-topped console table bearing a decanter of whisky and some tumblers.

'Take Mr Howard's parcel upstairs, Bishop.' It was the same deep, incisive voice that Howard had heard at the front door. He looked across the dimly lit room to see that the order had been given by an unusually handsome man seated on a settee, moving some magazines about in front of him as if he were playing a game. 'Go on, man – the parcel – upstairs.' He spoke with barely controlled patience this time, lifting his hand in a graceful gesture to indicate the direction Bishop should take.

When they were alone the man on the settee smiled faintly at Howard, shaking his head as a comment on the difficulty of getting simple instructions obeyed. 'I'm Roy Seymour. The general factotum here. Everything's in train. Help yourself to a drink. Magazine?' He spoke in the tone of one accustomed to being diplomatic and helpful but his super-bored expression did not invite conversation. A negligent smoothing of his lustrous black hair and he began to scan a copy of *Queen*.

Howard poured himself a glass of whisky and glanced discreetly at the faultless profile, ironically remembering a far-off period when he had wanted to look like that. He dissembled a yawn – after a long day a continuous effort to appear at ease was tiring; the central heating and liqueur whisky were thawing him out, and the faintly oppressive sensation of being a tourist in a palace was soporific too. He slumped down farther in the chair, letting his feet sink deep into the Pekin washed-silk carpet.

Looking round idly at the chinoiserie wallpaper with designs of flowering trees, giant ferns, and birds in blue, green, and grisaille on a pale pink background Howard wondered what it would be like to be employed in a household like this. Its organization was beyond his comprehension. Would there be some sort of shift system or did Bishop work exceedingly long hours on the understanding that any time he was not cross-questioning visitors he could spend in having a smoke or a cat-nap? And the 'general factotum' with the perfectly cut mohair suit, Eton Ramblers tie, and world-weary air – would he be at Mr Abacus's disposal all evening?

The door opened but instead of Bishop another Apollo, blond this time, appeared, calling out to Seymour: 'I say, where's the action, Roy? I keep hearing hoots of laughter but can't track them down. Rather frustrating. What gives?' He followed this up with some comic pantomime, raising his eyebrows, making stage Jewish grimaces and gestures; then he noticed Howard and immediately encompassed him in an actor's practised grin.

'Dave!' Roy Seymour exclaimed the name in a way that plainly demonstrated relief from tedium and got up to greet the blond man effusively, shepherding him quickly out of the room, turning back just as they went through the door to wave negligently at Howard: 'Won't be long now, I'm sure. Have another drink?'

Howard ignored the suggestion and took out his cheque-book, flipping through the stubs and making lightning calculations; it was compulsive, salutary reading. His bank manager would agree that he needed the fifty pounds he was going to make on the Morland book.

'Will you kindly follow me, sir?' In the intervening ten minutes Bishop's manner had changed perceptibly; he ushered Howard through the hall in an attentive way, turning at the stairs to grin reassuringly, like a dentist promising that nothing very painful lay ahead.

The music and laughter had stopped but on the next floor

Howard heard the distinctively light, youthful voice of Mr Abacus saying decisively: 'Well, it's time he learnt to act and speak *posément*.' When Bishop showed him through the door Howard experienced two surprises. First there was only one person in the room, so that it seemed the slightly threatening sentence had been rehearsed or spoken without an audience; secondly there was the momentary shock of seeing the tiny figure that greeted him with: 'Oh good, fine. Do come in, Howard.'

A manikin, about the size of a ten-year-old boy, was seated behind a very low Spanish mahogany desk, regarding him with grave brown eyes. It passed through Howard's mind how many times the abnormally small man must encounter surprise on meeting strangers and he was at once aware that he must give no sign of this. The large, rather fine brown eyes looked as if they would be particularly acute at detecting fleeting expressions.

'I was hoping you'd be kind enough to join me. Always have a snack at this time.' The little man indicated a plate bearing two green figs before him, and a tray with a bottle of Taittinger '59 Blanc de Blancs champagne and some tiny sandwiches that looked appropriate for a doll's tea-party.

Howard gazed down at the tray with genuine enthusiasm. The hospitality was welcome both because of his hunger and the chance it gave of making this interview easier. 'Thanks. That would be very nice. I seem to have missed a meal somewhere today ... er, Mr Abacus?'

The manikin snorted a mixture of amusement and derision: 'Sorry about that slight deception. Mine own poor joke. Abacus? Man first wrote on a board over which he sprinkled fine dust. Abacus, d'you see, from the Semitic a, b, q. No, my name's Curtis Mahon. But the pseudonym pleases me. Mr Dust ...'

Mahon left the sentence unfinished, hanging enigmatically in the air between them. He had the indefinable air of someone listening to a secret voice. After taking private counsel he leant across the desk and poured out two glasses of champagne; his movements were deft but Howard could see that they concealed a little awkwardness in dealing with the weight of the full bottle. Howard tried to imagine what it must be like to be a man immured in a child's body, to have such puny arms and legs, and, much more important for anyone sensitive, to know that one would be regarded by strangers as an oddity.

Mahon carefully dissected the purple-bloomed green fruit, exposing the curd-coloured flesh as if this was the first step in a surgical operation. He looked up, smiling at Howard and said: *'Erst kommt das Fressen und dann kommt der Moral.* Stuffing yourself comes first, moralizing after. By the way – do you play?' He indicated a Chinese ivory chess set at the end of the desk in which the Kings were nine inches high and the major pieces were mounted on intricate balls within balls.

Howard shook his head: 'No, alas – I'm afraid not. I've often thought I'd like to but never got around to learning. Pure laziness.'

A glint of amusement appeared momentarily in Mahon's eyes, then he stifled a yawn which gave his small face an odd, bleary look. It would have been easy to stare at him, to scrutinize the serene forehead, the unlined cheeks which showed no sign of ever being shaved, the tiny highly-arched fingernails and the hands which only differed from those of a child in being patterned with large pale freckles, but Howard was careful always to meet the concentrated gaze of Mahon's alert brown eyes, taking in details of his appearance only as he reached for a sandwich or his glass.

Chewing a piece of parsley Howard was puzzling over 'Mr Dust' and 'moralizing after'. Was this some kind of elaborate hoax after all? Had he been manoeuvred into buying the Morland book by a wealthy nut who was running a private purity campaign?

Mahon grinned, showing pearl-like teeth, and said, replying to Howard's unspoken doubts: 'Delighted, of course, with the book. A triumph! A veritable masterpiece!' He gestured vaguely and Howard noticed that the Morland book lay on a table by the wall. 'And, indeed, with the way in which you handled the deal. By the way, the price you are asking? I couldn't find an invoice.'

'The price agreed. Two-fifty.' Howard replied with a faint note of asperity as the thought struck him that now he had been

15

impressed with the set-up at Brooke House he was going to be asked to take less.

'That's fine. Many thanks. I only meant to imply that if you had been forced to pay more, then naturally I was willing to raise my price in turn.'

'Do you mind if I ask one question?' Having said this Howard paused for a moment; he had had more champagne than sandwiches and felt slightly vague, as if he could not marshal his thoughts quickly enough. 'I've been rather puzzled – about the book. I mean you knew of its existence and that the owner might sell it for two hundred pounds, yet you got Henry Bailey to suggest that I buy it on your behalf and charge you fifty pounds commission. Frankly I don't understand why Henry didn't arrange it for you. Or your secretary for that matter. If Mr Seymour had bought it direct you could have saved the fifty.'

Mahon rubbed his hands noiselessly. 'Glad you raised the point. Queen's Gambit in chess – unless one is a master player the Queen's Gambit, where a pawn is offered for sacrifice, is best declined. Myself I always query something for nothing. I'm distinctly uneasy if I can't see what's in it for the other fellow.'

Mahon turned to flash an appreciative look at one of the oil paintings on the wall to his left, a luscious backside by Boucher, as if this held a clue to his eccentric behaviour. 'The fact is I've been looking for some time for a dealer who would carry out occasional transactions for me. *Not*, I emphasize this to reassure you, just acquiring erotica. As a matter of fact it's only the great rarity, when the erotic happens to be a work of art, that appeals to me in that field. No, as a collector generally one sometimes hears of – well, desirable things, and it's always much better to make an approach through a professional. I like Henry Bailey – he's astute but he's firmly wedded to the medieval period and refuses to be dragged beyond the sixteenth century. Mind you he's been very wise to specialize. I've always thought that if one specialized in practically anything, mastered just one subject – became an authority on, say, bauxite . . .'

Howard's attention wandered a little. He had received similar advice from other rich men: simple precepts which they knew he was incapable of following. His eyes alighted on the Boucher nude, the damson-coloured curtains, a bull's-eye window with a gilded grill and a statue in a corner, a winged Eros passionately embracing a naked Psyche who yielded, falling back.

'... of course the real trick is to keep on wanting something. We want nothing till we have been *cheated* out of it...' Mahon's face clouded momentarily. 'So it follows we get nothing till we have stopped wanting it.'

Howard was thinking of how much Mahon had been cheated by a caprice of Nature when, as if to underline this point, the manikin got down awkwardly from his chair. Standing up he looked even smaller and, by some absurd prejudice, it was difficult to take someone of his stature seriously. He walked across the room and laid a hand lovingly on the frame of another picture. 'Do you admire Rossetti? For me he is *the* psychologist of love, the *mal sacré*... He saw in woman the embodiment of man's longing to escape from the triviality of daily life to the fount of eternal beauty...'

Before Howard could express his admiration for the striking Rossetti portrait of the girl holding a peacock-feather fan Mahon was moving quickly across the room again with tiny, bird-like steps. Apropos of nothing he muttered, 'Don't get out much.' This was thrown away and obviously not intended for comment. 'But I track down desirable things,' he added defensively. 'Just give me some facts and I can do a lot with them. Everything has to do with facts!'

Mahon swung round suddenly with a challenging expression: his large eyes glittered with intelligence and Howard was deeply impressed by the formidable qualities of this little brooding recluse; he could understand now how Brooke House had been acquired.

'The idea that imagination has nothing to do with facts? *Pseudoxia epidemica*. Imagination's very stuff? Facts.' Mahon briefly washed his hands in mid-air. 'Together we could pull off some coups. Are you on? Working part-time for me? I think you would find it a profitable arrangement.'

Howard nodded. Despite Mahon's disclaimer Howard suspected that the collection was mainly to do with the '*mal sacré*', but his own morality was flexible, based simply on a reluctance to hurt people. He had no objection to becoming an agent for

17

the rather pathetic manikin, imprisoned by his thwarting circumstances. What harm could a collection of erotica do anyone?

A glint of amusement appeared in Mahon's eyes and then was dowsed. 'Do you have an invoice for the Morland book?'

Howard hesitated and Mahon nodded sagely: 'Ah, the legal mind! But no need to worry. There's been no contravention of the Post Office Act of 1953 and I'm quite at liberty to make a collection of erotica if I so choose. However we'll keep any such transactions as informal as possible. You'll find that "Mr Abacus" will always pay in cash. Just scribble a signature on this receipt. That's purely book-keeping for my files which are *not* open to inspection by Her Majesty's Department of Inland Revenue or anyone else for that matter.' He handed Howard a Lloyd's Bank blue printed envelope with a heavy red seal. 'Three hundred pounds. The extra fifty as a retainer to pay for any time you may spend on working on projects for me which don't come off. I have something up my sleeve ... I know where there are some *very* interesting diaries and perhaps you can get the owner to disgorge. But more of that another day.'

Mahon moved up close so that Howard was aware of a distinctive sweet smell like caramel or vanilla, and ushered him out of the room, holding Howard's arm in an intimate way, breaking off at the door to make a dramatic gesture at the Boucher nude. 'Oh woman, woman, to fall into thine arms and not into thy hands,' he quoted. It sounded like a well-rehearsed party piece, but he gave Howard a searching look as if the warning might have a particular significance for him.

2

Howard walked quickly till he was out of sight of anyone watching from Brooke House then paused irresolutely. He had often felt like this, a boat without a rudder, since his wife Meg had died, and it was worse now that his daughter was living in France. The last few years of the marriage had not been happy but having a family had given his life an illusion of purpose which it lacked now. He stared down at a bird's cuneate footprints in a thin scattering of snow, lacking the desire to put one foot in front of the other. Alone he once more became morose and introspective. He had to call on his mother some time during the evening but did not feel like doing so in this restless, unsatisfactory mood.

'Don't get out much.' Howard could hear Mahon muttering this as though he had to explain or apologize for his circumscribed existence. Four words casually thrown away, yet they were the key to Mahon's life. Little 'Mr Dust' was a captive both of his freakish stature and the consequent frustration of his sexual drive, serving out his sentence in that slightly bizarre room decorated with sapphic figurines and sensuous paintings, poring over books with lascivious illustrations, all the inescapable paraphernalia of his unassuageable desire.

Howard slid his hand into the inner pocket of his jacket to trace out the satisfying shape of the sealed envelope; it was reassuring to find that it had not disappeared like fairy gold. 'Together we can pull off some coups.' How odd it would be to work even 'part-time' for that eccentric little millionaire: detached, effaced, concealed in the anonymous clothing of his dark suit, Howard would be like the agent of some scheming medieval prince. Well, that was how it seemed after whisky and champagne; no doubt a seedier picture would emerge when it was developed in the cold light of morning.

A three-quarter moon shone down from a completely clear sky glittering with stars, casting a curiously livid light on Carlton House Terrace which stretched before him and a small patch of grass with two trees on his right, leading to St James's Park. Close at hand he could see the frosted catherine wheels of spiders' webs on bushes and the armour of rime on the trees sparkled like tinsel. Farther away, across the Mall, the moonlight outlined the impressive bleak landscape of London in the grip of winter.

'Oh sod it!' Behind him Howard heard a young woman's voice swearing as if in desperation, then skittering footsteps. He turned just as a girl rushed past, with a muffled blasphemous exclamation which he could not take in properly. She was tall and slim, dressed in an absurdly short yellow coat and shiny black boots. She had banged into his shoulder running in pell-mell fashion and was obviously in distress of some kind, either drunk or ill. As he watched she stopped short, raising her arms in front of her as though she was struggling with an unseen assailant, then stumbled on shaking her head from side to side.

Howard sprinted to catch up with the girl as she reached the steps by the George VI statue; she was leaning forward as if she might fall down them at any moment. He could not make out whether she was drunk or hysterical. She had very long straight black hair. He came up to her, smelling whisky, and looked into myopic, aquamarine eyes. 'Oh God ... Get out of the way!' she said in a shaky voice. 'Can't you see I'm going to be sick!'

Howard put his right arm firmly round her high thin shoulders and held her forehead with his left hand. 'Go on then – be sick! I just don't want you to fall down those steps.'

The girl struggled in his arms, threshing about like a frightened animal; she swallowed, gulped, and retched loudly, but only a thin trickle of bitter-smelling bile came from her mouth. The yellow stuff made Howard heave slightly but he held on tightly, looking away above the trees in the park. Somewhere close at hand a cat was mewing piteously. The girl was trembling but the convulsive movements dictated by the desire to vomit gradually stopped, and he could tell the fit of nausea was passing.

The girl shook her head slowly from side to side then gave him a defiant look. 'You see ... But I did warn you. You shouldn't have ... Is there any on your hand?' She gulped again and retched weakly without bringing anything up. When she smoothed the hair from her forehead he glimpsed a butterfly tattooed on her right wrist. She sighed deeply and said 'Oh – pukesville.'

Howard took out a handkerchief and wiped her mouth. 'Finished?'

'I don't know.' She gave him a quizzical look and smiled weakly. 'Why? Are you tired of this samaritan lark?'

'No, but if you have I'm going to get rid of this. Well I'm going to anyway.' Howard balled up the handkerchief and threw it behind the statue. 'Whoever finds it will think there's been some odd kind of pilgrimage, a lèse-majesté ritual...' He indicated the effigy of George VI looking mildly out over the park. 'It's okay. I've got another one if there's an emergency.'

'I say, I *am* impressed. One for the show and one for blow, eh!' The girl gave a crooked grin then shivered, and her teeth chattered uncontrollably. Even with a sickly pale complexion and mussed hair she was extremely attractive. Howard rubbed her hands roughly between his and said, 'Are you going to be all right now? Shall I push off?'

'No – don't go *now*. Before was when you should have gone. My legs are like jelly and I can use a strong right arm.' She pointed in the direction of some parked cars. 'Are you motorized?'

'Sorry, no, but I can easily nip down to Waterloo Place and get you a taxi.'

'No need. I was wondering if you could just walk with me across the park. I haven't far to go, but on rubber legs . . .'

'Of course I'll walk a bit. Where to?'

She waved an arm vaguely. 'Directly across. Go to gaol. Go directly to gaol. Do *not* collect £200.'

When they had crossed the Mall and were walking on a footpath in the park she sniffed her hands and said: 'Oh Lord! *The* new drink. Whisky and vomit. Wait a sec!' She bent down and washed her face and hands in the snow. 'Ah, that's better. Much better! I don't feel bad now. In fact quite good! How odd it is about being sick, you know – once it's finished,' she shrugged, 'it's finished. But then I must say in self-defence I hadn't been making a pig of myself or anything like that. It was just a case of one too many whiskies on an empty stomach. Yep – I'm okay now.'

Rather reluctantly Howard disengaged his hand from her arm. 'Well I'll go then.' There was something very attractive and appealing about her youth and lack of inhibition. Somehow it seemed perfectly natural to be walking along talking to her, and once he had left her life would seem empty and hollow again.

'I say! Aren't you the dour old samaritan figure then! What does the rule-book say? Help victim only while absolutely essential?' She reached out an ice-cold hand and took his. 'You can see I still need a bit of warmth and comfort.'

Close-to her pale face, scrubbed clean by the snow of make-up apart from one blurred streak of eye-liner, was exciting. Her coarse black hair had a bluish tinge in the moonlight; her thick, arched brows outlined the blue-green eyes dramatically. He could not tell whether the extra rapid fluttering of her dark eye-lids was a come-on or simply nervous reaction.

They stood still looking at each other in silence for a few moments. She made no attempt to disguise her short-sighted inspection of his eyes and mouth. Then she giggled: 'I *think* you look rather nice but the joke is I can't really tell without my specs. Everything's a bit blurry. When I get you under a strong light you may turn out quite horrid. Perhaps that's why you were so ready to help with the – sick.'

Howard laughed. Her gaiety was infectious and he felt almost light-hearted, as if he'd suddenly thrown off the tedious routine and trappings that made up his life in a cul-de-sac. 'Yes, per-haps that's it.'

The girl ducked her head nervously and held out her hand to be shaken in a manner that was slightly old-fashioned and formal, contradicting her language. 'Jill – Jill Lammas.'

'Nicholas Howard.' After the exchange of names there was an awkward silence. It seemed as if the introduction had banished the intimacy that had sprung up between them so quickly, and now they were left with nothing to say. They stared at the ice on the lake and then moved slowly on to the low bridge to watch the antics of the ducks fussing about at the edge of a patch of black water. Jill sighed again and looked up into the sky, sniffing in the clear night air.

'Ah, that's wonderful. If you just concentrate on the sky... Keep staring hard and after a minute or so you can absolutely feel this funny old world spinning along. Whirling on forever but going nowhere. How very strange it all is!' She took his arm firmly as they walked along again, and he was excited by this and the way in which the pressure of her fingers grew stronger at times like a cat clawing. He was intensely aware of her thin body intermittently brushing his – he had been even when she was in the throes of vomiting. Was physical attraction for him simply a matter of propinquity? A few minutes in her company seemed to have obliterated his feelings of guilt over Meg. Would his futile longing, the hopeless love he professed for Catherine Gurney, similarly be forgotten just because this strange young girl was holding his arm tightly, her fingers exploring the end of his sleeve, fiddling with his watch strap.

'Are you married?' She had turned round suddenly to face him as if she could not depend on the validity of the answer without seeing his reactions.

With his free hand he rubbed the back of his neck. It was a nervous habit he had when tired or pent-up. 'I was. My wife died. Last year. Just before Christmas ...' He stopped confusedly, not sure how much information to give her. She was easy to talk to and he felt it would be wonderful to unburden himself of some of his doubts and fears about Meg's death. It might be possible to say things to her that had been bottled up ever since that terrible day; yet, simultaneously he was aware of the absurdity of contemplating such confessions to a chance acquaintance. He made a vague gesture as a prelude to saying something, but the words did not come.

Jill was watching him with a cool, judging look – she seemed to be weighing schemes which she had no intention of imparting to him. She murmured 'I'm sorry' and ran her fingers lightly over the back of his hand, but when she spoke again the conventional tone of sympathy had vanished: 'Well, hands up all those who want a cup of coffee.'

Mentioning Meg's death had reminded Howard of the absolute gulf between the living and the dead; his inward eye projected the last snapshot it had taken of her ('Died not there; no sight or sound again'). When he felt Jill's hand tugging urgently at his own it was as if he was waking from a disturbing dream. She walked quicker and quicker as they left Birdcage Walk and then began to scamper along one of the small streets behind St James's Park station. The physical release of running willy-nilly over slippery pavements cancelled out his thoughts. Abruptly Jill stopped and bobbed her head to a passer-by. 'Evening, Father!' She spoke to a fat unhealthy-looking priest waddling along. As soon as he had passed she burst into laughter. 'Do you know what he really worships? It's food, mate! He's always in our local Chinese caff. Downs about a dozen dishes and has chips with it. It's a horrible scene!'

Howard was occupied in studying Jill as they walked along. She had high cheek bones which gave her face a rather taut look, a short tilted nose, and a wide mouth. She walked with a slightly awkward, coltish gait, holding her arms straight down. She was five foot five or six, about twenty years old. It was like being out with one of his daughter's friends. He tried to think of something to say but it seemed unlikely that his narrow interests would be shared by her and he kept rejecting phrases as they formed. Finally he uttered a stilted sentence: 'It's funny to be trudging through all this snow and slush – in about thirty-six hours I shall be in the heat of the tropics – the West Indies.'

Jill turned to look at him closely with an odd expression; momentarily sadness clouded her eyes and when she spoke there was a note of forced gaiety: 'I say I say! I've heard of place-dropping but this is ridiculous. A likely story. What are you doing here then? You should be home packing or something.'

'No, it's a lightning trip. In and out, there and back on connecting flights. I – my wife – she owned a tiny house in Grenada. It was left to her by her parents. Now I'm selling it and I want to see it first. I've never been there.'

'Ah, I see. Checking up that the price is right. Well – how exciting for you! I wish I was going off somewhere glamorous, or anywhere in fact. I love travelling of any kind. Even dull old train journeys – I always wish they would never end. You see I like the idea of destroying bridges once they're crossed ... So – you are a member of the landed gentry, selling up the West Indies estate. I'm feeling continually more hesitant about showing you my poor shack.'

She paused and looked closely again at Howard with a serious expression, then shook her head as if rejecting some idea. Howard was puzzled as to what could be going on in her mind.

'Do you know what I like about the world?' she asked rhetorically. 'That it's all a mystery. Nobody knows what's what! Even which side is up. And that's a fact! There aren't any rules. You know – live today, there's no tomorrow. Come on, Don Giovanni, this is it.'

They had stopped before a tall, dark, and rather forbidding house. There were six bell-pushes by the front door frame. From an upper window there was the sound of pop music, the Jimi Hendrix Experience's 'Blue Haze'. Jill paused in her struggle to fit a key into a dodgy-looking lock and said, 'I warn you I shall put on my specs to have a proper dekko at you once we're in.'

The battered door opened reluctantly to disclose an ill-lit hallway. Jill flashed him a defiant look: 'How very average, he exclaimed. Oh billiard balls! My milk's gone. What a swiz!' She rat-tatted on a door to the left and then pressed her ear up against it. 'He's in there all right the miserable old sod, skinning flints. Quiet as a mouse. He only comes to life when I switch on my record-player. Then straight away he's banging on my door, shouting out "Turn off that po music . . ." '

The door on which Jill had been leaning was opened and a small man with a thick thatch of grey hair and dark bloodshot eyes appeared. He stared rebelliously at Jill.

Jill made a perfunctory movement with her hand to introduce the two men. 'Mr Russell – Mr Howard. Sorry to bother you but I wondered – about my milk. It doesn't seem to be there.'

Russell shrugged his shoulders. 'Well, I don't know. I definitely put it there.'

Jill grimaced and sighed. 'Oh – how frustrating. Some people! Okay, sorry.' She turned round to Howard: 'Then it will just have to be black coffee, or white with whatnot. You know, tinned.'

She ignored Russell, who continued to stare as though they were visitors from Mars, and opened a light blue door on which the paint had run down in streaks, leaving some thick blobs. 'Won't you come into my parlour? But you must promise not to pass out with the luxury thereof.'

Jill's bed-sittingroom, bathed in pink light, looked rather like a stall in a fairground. It was cluttered with so many decorations and ornaments that the eye could not take them in all at once. On a facing wall there was a striking, full-length portrait of a woman in Edwardian dress holding a parasol, and a large photograph of Greta Garbo in profile. Japanese kites, plastic balls, and mobiles quivered on strings suspended from the ceiling. The walls were papered with a severe narrow white and silver stripe but this was largely covered with drawings, photographs, framed poems, and quotations. Howard noticed a snapshot of a big dog dressed up in coat and trousers with a pipe stuck in its mouth, then glimpsed his own tired-looking face and wary grey eyes in a cheval-glass. How out of place he must look in this gay, youthful ambience!

Jill bent down over some dolls on the couch-bed and murmured to them soothingly. She picked up an old bear which had lost most of its stuffing. 'Teddy Bear, am I heartless?' she asked, holding him in front of her and gazing intently into the black, glass eyes. 'Am I really heartless?' Still holding the bear in one hand she struck a few random notes on a toy piano then swung round picking up candy-floss pink spectacles to confront Howard. 'Definitely *not* horrid. Rather nice in fact.' She walked over to him and stood very close, placing her hand against his cheek. 'Just a teeny bit battered perhaps – you know, a little beat-up beneath the eyes.' Now that she was so near, Howard could smell the lingering trace of honeysuckle perfume round her neck. 'But that's all right, darling.'

She turned away, taking off her boots and then her coat, opening the zipper on her dress in an absent-minded way, changing into a dressing-gown, not troubling to hide herself. The glimpses of her young body were at once tantalizing and vaguely upsetting to Howard: he experienced a sudden sinking feeling, the sensation that he was out of his depth, embarked on something he could not handle. It was strange the way this girl appeared for no reason to think that he was an experienced amorist, a 'Don Giovanni'. If she knew that the only affair he had experienced in twenty years of marriage was a platonic one, consisting of clandestine letters and phone-calls, hand-holding, and a few stolen kisses!

In stockinged feet Jill was about four or five inches shorter than Howard and she stood on tiptoe to try a cool, experimental kiss. Desire came on him like a trance; he bent down and the kiss became a lingering one in which their tongues met. They clung together so that he could feel every inch of her body. In the silence Howard could hear only the faint jangling noise of some brass strips moving in a breeze that occasionally parted the curtain.

After long minutes she pulled away. 'Mm – yes – strictly dreams department – I must just wash my face properly then I'll be back for more.'

She disappeared through a white door into a surprisingly neat, uncluttered bathroom. Howard took off his overcoat and stood fiddling with a large, garishly painted wooden popgun. There was an old-fashioned gas-fire and when he bent down to light it he noticed a layer of soot behind, an odd cushiony growth like black moss.

He went over to read a quotation in a black frame: 'Love is a farce invited by nature to fool men and women into propagating their species – Strindberg.' Beneath this there was another one cut from a toy catalogue and ringed round in blue pencil: 'This doll really does kiss. Hold close to the cheek and when her arms are squeezed, she'll give a big kiss. Conforms to British Standards.'

The bathroom door opened and Jill appeared with bare feet and holding her robe at the neck in such a way that Howard felt sure she was wearing nothing beneath it. She seemed nervous, staring at him with her face slightly screwed up as if she was looking into a bright light. 'We won't bother with coffee, shall we, darling? We'll soon warm each other up.'

Howard shook his head from side to side, undecided what to say or do. Casual promiscuous love-making was something he had not experienced before. It was wrong of course to go to bed with a girl half his age just because he lusted after her and she seemed to want him. He tried to summon up the will to get out of this situation and a phrase to make her understand why he had to leave, but when he did speak it was simply as if their ages were reversed and he was a youth being seduced by a determined matron: 'No, really, I ought to go.'

This piffling pusillanimity amused Jill and banished any hesitation on her part. She came towards him laughing: 'I say, aren't you the nervous one! Is this kind of thing against your insurance or something? Pull the curtains, darling – we'll just have the moonlight.'

When he turned from the window she had come right up against him and he bent down into the web of scent about her neck, pulling the robe open, kissing her shoulders. She made

27

little whimpering noises as his lips touched her breasts and whispered 'Darling' again and again as his hands went round her back, first holding her very tight and then slowly, gently, exploring. After a while he held her arms and pushed her back towards the couch. Their mutual desire was indeed a trance – love's trance that was like Sleeping Beauty magic. They would lie together, journeying in the dream-like world of desire and lose themselves. Everything else would be forgotten and it would be moonlight always.

3

'Do you want to hear a dirty joke...?' Howard looked round uneasily. After their love-making he and Jill had fallen asleep, then he had woken with a start remembering that his mother was expecting him and would be worrying if he failed to appear by ten o'clock. Finding it was twenty minutes to eleven he had hurriedly pulled on his clothes, kissing Jill good-bye with a whispered explanation about the preparations he had to make for going to Grenada the next day which she had probably not absorbed in her drowsy state. He now lived above his London business premises so he had scribbled a note on one of his cards, underlined the phone number, and propped it up on the table. Coming directly from the warm bed to the cold street had made him feel low and slightly queasy. It was distinctly unnerving to be suddenly posed this question about a dirty joke, particularly as the disembodied voice came from an odd angle, high above his left shoulder.

As Howard swivelled round the question was completed: 'About the Queen?' An owl-eyed man, about six foot three or four in height, was grinning at him in an unpleasantly derisive way. Howard looked the big man up and down coolly, as if he was a tree due to be felled. Howard had been taught to box in the Army by an instructor who had twenty years experience of fighting in fairground booths; he knew a lot of ways of escaping punishment and was not unduly worried about being involved in trouble if it was forced upon him. He shook his head slowly from side to side and replied 'Not particularly' in a frosty voice.

'All right, cobber. Just a friendly question, that's all.' The owl-eyed man gave a mirthless laugh. 'Only trying to be matey like, see. Christ! You limeys, you reely are stand-offish aren't yer?'

The big man's Australian accent was either more exaggerated than any Howard had previously experienced or bogus. A primitive smile revealed dingy teeth but did not alter a bleak, sadistic gaze. Howard could imagine how a mouse must feel seeing an owl staring down prior to the shriek and the swoop.

When the smile vanished the man's tone became even more aggrieved. 'I'm on duty, you know, out in all this f—ing snow and snot,' he whined. 'Not like some who're pleasure bound. But I ain't complainin'. We don't you see. Oh no, not in the service. If someone has it really tough, gets killed say, well we just say, "F— his luck. He shouldn't have joined if he couldn't take a joke..."'

It was the big man's turn to look Howard up and down and he did it with a knowing grin, to such effect that Howard glanced down to see if any buttons apart from those on his overcoat were undone. All was in order. He shifted from foot to foot, hardly heeding the monologue. He did not for one moment believe that this man was in the police and that presumably was what he was expected to think with the references to being 'on duty' and 'the service'. He had no intention of being intimidated or long detained by this big oaf. He said, 'Well, I must be off. Simply got to get out of this "f—ing snow and snot".' He permitted himself a grim smile. They stared at each other for a few moments silently so that Howard could hear the other's stertorous breathing. The big man moved his powerful shoulders restlessly, then brushed off some invisible object from his left sleeve; he flourished a hand that looked like a boxing-glove and reached for Howard's shoulder. 'I'm not in the police. Not any more,' he admitted with a frankness that lacked any appeal.

With an inward sigh of relief Howard spotted a taxi cruising along Petty France. Its lit-up 'For Hire' sign appeared unusually attractive, like a harbour after a tricky voyage. He side-stepped the owl-eyed man, eluded the out-stretched arm, calling out 'Got to go. Mustn't miss that,' and sprinted up the road.

When Howard turned round to stare back through the taxi's rear window he saw that the big man had vanished. It wasn't so unusual to come across human oddities in London, particularly at night when they seemed to abound in the main line railway stations, and he did not give the encounter another thought.

While he looked out at the lights strung across Constitution Hill an image was forming on a mental screen of Jill, as she had appeared with her long black hair spread in disarray on the pillow. In the moon's lurid light her eyes looked violet green, her face thin and wan. When she had reached her climax it had been a violent one in which she kept throwing back her head with her arms outstretched, opening her mouth as if she was shouting soundlessly. Then there had been some muttered pillow talk, and she had suddenly slid off into sleep half-way through an incomprehensible sentence about salt kisses.

As he watched her asleep, Howard had experienced a feeling of tenderness for this strange girl whom he had met and taken in one evening. Before that moment there had only been desire – a selfish, demanding, partly aggressive feeling. But asleep with her dark head cradled on his arm Jill appeared touchingly immature, as defenceless and innocent as a child. Suddenly there had been all sorts of questions he had wanted to ask her, about her past, her family, what she hoped for from life, and it was frustrating that she was walled away in sleep's kingdom. A real concern for someone approached his mature idea of love – a self-forgetful concentration on another's true being and happiness, such as he had felt for Catherine Gurney.

What bitter irony it was, as things had turned out, that it had been his wife Meg who had first met Catherine, Meg who had persisted in arranging a further meeting, Meg who had nurtured a growing friendship between themselves and Catherine and Toby. He could remember quite clearly how Meg had first described Catherine whom she had met at an art gallery cocktail party in King Street: 'Very natural and gay. Full of life. Striking eyes, deep brown, curved at the bottom edges'. Then he had met Catherine and gradually a feeling of attraction between them had grown and been revealed in furtive hand-holding on a joint theatre visit, leading eventually to secret telephone calls and their subsequent few meetings alone when they had just walked and talked.

Howard sighed, slumped in his seat, and shut his eyes. For perhaps the hundredth time he was mentally reviewing the evening of the firework party at the Gurney's house in the previous November. It was a miserable but irresistible expedition into the past, one he knew that he was doomed to take again and again. Once more he walked with Meg on a smoky dark evening from Earls Court Station to Tregunter Road, getting there rather late to find the ritualistic proceedings well under way with Toby Gurney apparently in his element, in fisherman's sweater and wellington boots, supervising the lighting of rockets and the larger Roman Candles at the bottom of the garden. Howard had stood about feeling rather bored, pleased to escape when he was asked to find some matches. Going back into the house he had come across Catherine watching from the french windows in a darkened room. Catherine's face had been flushed from the bonfire and when he glimpsed her eyes they appeared preternaturally large and lustrous. They had stood, arms around each other, looking out at the fireworks' kaleidoscopic lights for some minutes without a word. Then they had kissed and she had said, 'You know I love you'. At that moment, as if on cue, Meg had come into the room, switching on the light. He could see her face as she entered, scrutinize yet again her faintly bewildered expression.

Now he felt certain that the air of natural intimacy between Catherine and himself must have been unmistakable, but the incident seemed at the time to have passed off as being of little importance. Meg had made some joking comment about having returned in the nick of time. But who could tell what her true feelings were, what impression had lodged, how suspicions had grown from that moment? And once suspicion was planted how easily, by a yawn, an inclined head, a flash of emotion, one could be unmasked.

Certainly during the following weeks Meg had become increasingly edgy – sometimes so strung up and bad tempered that he felt an incautious word on his part might lead to an orgy of recrimination in which an accumulation of resentment would be

31

unloaded. Their relationship had been an unsatisfactory one for years which had seen a gradual divergence of their natures and interests, but never before had he given her any reason for jealousy. Their marriage had just become, like so many others, a matter of habit without much feeling on either side. At the first sign of reciprocation from Catherine he had wanted to give her an undemanding devotion, to nurse an incorruptible dream of love.

That it was a hopeless dream he had known from the first – Catherine had three young children and he had no intention of ruining their lives for a feeling that might vanish as quickly as it had come. So his sensation of being in a cul-de-sac had evolved: partly no doubt the middle-aged impression of being on a tread-mill and having to run all the time to keep where you were, but mainly the daunting, abiding knowledge that his love for Catherine was doomed to come to nothing. He thought he had hidden his feelings from Meg, certainly he had tried to, but throughout November and December she had been increasingly tense and had hit out at him with acute criticisms: 'You worry me, Nick. Aren't you ever going to take anything seriously?' 'A bitter joke – that's your answer to everything.'

On several occasions he had been the guilty witness of her uneasy ruminant moments. Once on a walk along the river from Henley he had felt that she was on the verge of saying something, determined at last to drag matters into the open, but the moment had passed and he had been glad to escape. Gutless he thought. Perhaps if he hadn't been a coward, had faced up to the situation, everything would have been different.

With a deep feeling of remorse Howard remembered the last time he had seen Meg alive. It had been on December 18th at Paddington Station, crowded with Christmas shoppers. He was going to a book-sale at Sotheby's, she was supposed to be meeting a friend to shop in Knightsbridge. He had turned away to hear her call 'Nick – Wait!' in an impassioned voice. He faced about, noting with pity the dark signs of sleeplessness beneath her eyes but dreading the revelation that might be going to take place at last. Her expression of vagueness when they had waved good-bye had been replaced by one of sharp attention. 'Nick – will you do something for me?' She had spoken with suppressed eagerness as if her request was of great importance. 'Yes, of course. What is it?' He had replied in a matter of fact voice but was deeply uneasy. Not here, not now, he had thought. Then her expression had changed again – a hopeless look came into her eyes and the way she stood and moved her hands expressed dejection. It was as if her appeal had been rejected. Her lips formed a soundless word, then she said, 'No. It's nothing, not important. Don't bother. You must get off.'

Howard's two most vivid visual memories would always be of Meg on that fateful day, the 18th December. A mental cinema flashed them on at random moments, to disconcert and mortify him, to impress on him again the meaning of the word remorse. First as she stood under the clock at Paddington Station, in her dark blue coat, nervously fiddling with her handbag – looking lost and purposeless among the hurrying, jostling crowd, as though she was rooted to the spot and might still be there when he returned that evening to catch the train for Henley. Then the shockingly vivid yet unreal glimpse he had of her dead body twelve hours later in the Charing Cross Hospital. The *Evening News*'s brief paragraph had slanted the affair as if it was an accident 'CHRISTMAS SHOPPING TRAGEDY. Woman falls on line. Horrified Christmas shoppers crowded on Oxford Circus platform 2 witnessed . . .' and the coroner's jury had returned an open verdict. There was no suicide note or any evidence that it had not been an accident, and he was the only person in the world who knew what was more likely to be the truth. He could forget it now and then as he could blot out the terrifying picture of Meg going down before the train, crushed to the rails, but such recurring images and memories were to be his punishment. He had escaped any public reproof, had known only sympathy, but privately he had received his sentence, a life-long intermittent one of guilt and repentance.

'You see. I got you there!' The taxi-driver had turned round to speak through the glass division in a tone of self-congratulation about his smooth driving on hazardous roads. 'But that's it! No more for this kiddy! No sir! Half-an-hour from now I shall be all tucked up in beddy-bies.'

Howard nodded and gratefully handed him a ten shilling

note. There were no lights at the front of his mother's house and this probably meant she had got tired of waiting and was finding some job to do in the kitchen. She had given him a key when he had shut up his house near Henley, and as he used it to open the front door he experienced a strange sensation that time was in flux – that when he passed through the hall he might find his mother as she had been when he returned from school in the 1930s, or coming on leave from the Army in the 1940s. The furniture was modest but of good quality and dateless – little had been altered about the house as far back as he remembered; even minor changes had come to a stop with the death of his father eight years before. Now his mother seemed to live a life of perpetually waiting, always concerned for him and his daughter Jacqueline. She had written a weekly letter to Jacqueline since she had been at the Sorbonne.

There was a smell of polish in the hall but also a delicious fragrance which he tracked down to a blue bowl of narcissi and ivy leaves.

'Nick! I thought you said nine!'

'I know. I'm sorry. Got held up. Some last minute things to deal with. But my bag's packed, all ready to be collected in the morning. I thought I'd stay here tonight if that's okay.'

She dismissed this request as superfluous with a little familiar gesture of her fingers. 'I've been worrying a bit – about your trip to Grenada. All that expense, Nick! You told me money was tight just now. There's the house at Henley – is that still on your hands, and the shop not let? And your new London shop. Jacqueline ... I can't imagine how you're managing. Can I help?'

'It's all right, Mother. It's true my overdraft's reached an all-time high, but once I sell the Grenada house I shall have plenty of funds. This trouble is just temporary. The bank knows that. I shall certainly get rid of the lease on the shop in Henley soon, and the house there is just hanging fire because of the weather. Places right on the river look their least attractive in midwinter.' His mother had been used to his father's Civil Service salary with the prospect of a good pension – his own livelihood depending on selling old books must seem extremely precarious to her, and he was used to her periodical bouts of worrying about his prospects.

His mother looked unconvinced but said: 'Well at least it will make a nice break for you.'

'Not much of one, alas. Only two days there, about five days with the flights.'

'Two days. All those thousands of miles, and – what was it – about two hundred pounds, just for two days! I didn't dream it was going to be as short as that.'

'Well, I'm not going on a holiday, Mother. Don't feel like it, and can't afford the time or the extra expense either. I simply want to check that the price Mr Quincy Adams advises me to take for the house there seems reasonable.'

'But will you be able to tell about that?'

'I don't say I shall be able to gauge it very closely, but I want to have a look. I do think it would be madness to sell a house without ever seeing it. A walk round the place and a chat to Mr Adams and I'll know better whether I want to sell. I get the feeling from his letters that he's a nice chap, and Meg liked him.' Howard handed his mother the last letter he had received from Quincy Adams on the attractive 'Carib Estates Inc., St George's' headed paper.

'So that's all you'll do there? I just can't get over you flying all that way for such a short visit. Meg had such a good holiday there ...' His mother hesitated and Howard knew she had regretted that sentence. 'And wasn't there a special reduced price on a three week trip?'

'Yes, I know. There still is.' Howard detected in his own voice the faint hint of tried patience he had heard when Roy Seymour gave instructions to the houseman Bishop at Brooke House. He saw his mother was rocking herself back and forward, a vulnerable look in her eyes. He could not imagine living a selfless life as she did. He remembered her clutching at his hand after Meg's funeral, saying lost bewildered hopeless things. He went over and kissed her forehead.

'Now don't you worry. A quick trip will suit me best in every way. You see, young Evans can look after the shop for a week but I don't know about leaving it to him for longer than that. And then I can cram a lot into two days, you know. By the way,

I've got to look up one of Meg's Grenadian friends, Nancy Douce. Did Meg ever mention her to you?'

'Yes, I remember the name. That was the young woman Meg liked so much. About twenty, I think. She said they got on very well despite the gap in their ages. Wasn't Miss Douce supposed to come and stay with you?'

'That's why I'm going to call on her, if I can. Meg said she would be staying with us in the autumn, then Nancy got a job in London and the idea was dropped apparently. Anyway I didn't hear any more about it and I've found some letters at Henley sent on from a London address for Nancy. I went round to the London address, in Bina Gardens, and the landlord said Nancy had left there – thought she might be coming on to Henley. A real mix-up. Then I found two of Nancy's books that she had apparently lent to Meg. So I'll return those at the same time.'

'What kind of books? Do you need to bother? Perhaps they were a present from Miss Douce. Are they heavy?'

Howard divined an unspoken little idea that lay behind his mother's questions. 'Not heavy enough for me to have to pay excess luggage, if that's what you mean. You ought to see my case. One light-weight pair of trousers, a few shirts and underclothes. I could take half a dozen books. Kind of books? Oh, one called *The Magus*, and the other *The Tarot*, both on magic. It's not a subject of mine but I do know that the Tarot is a pack of cards, dating from ancient times, used for fortune-telling, that kind of thing.'

'That's odd. I had no idea Meg was interested in magic.'

'I don't think she was. Maybe Nancy Douce wanted to lend them and Meg was too polite to say no.'

Howard wanted this conversation to end, so he rubbed his face with his hands then opened his eyes very wide as though he was having trouble keeping them open. It had the predictable effect of getting his mother out of her chair and off to fill a hot water-bottle. When she had gone, Howard brooded on the fact that he really had no idea if Meg might have become interested in magic. At one time it seemed as if they had exhausted every subject in the continual non-stop duologue that makes up marriage, but in the last year their conversation had been largely superficial and purely to do with every-day things. And then there were inevitably gaps in knowing about other people's ideas. It seemed more and more to him that everything in life was shifting, uncertain. He had no faith in Curtis Mahon's 'facts'. In his experience most so-called 'facts' were mere will-o'-the-wisps.

4

'Life is a dream, a little more coherent than most.' This quotation returned to Howard from time to time on his flight to Grenada. It had first come into his mind during the speedy transition from the metallic landscape of London, steel buildings against the leaden sky, to the apparently endless azure that waited for them just above the clouds; other stages of his journey repeated this theme. He had travelled a lot in Europe, but during the over-night stay at Barbados everything was strange and unfamiliar. Half-asleep in a taxi he had been whisked along narrow lanes beside fields of tall sugar-cane, past wooden shanties that looked as if they had just been improvised and ramshackle shops dramatically lit by petrol lamps. It was like seeing an ever-changing stage in the theatre. There were fireflies against a deep violet sky, bats hanging in trees like blighted fruit, people who called out gaily but moved with a kind of mournful listlessness and looked at him with eyes at once furtive and bold. There was the sickly sweet smell of the tropics, in which heavy flower perfumes were mixed with the occasional raw odours of untreated sewage. A few hours after the bitter winds and ash-grey sky of the metropolis there was soft warm air and the pervasive atmosphere of a dreamy creole idleness. When he got out of the taxi at the Lu-Mar Inn Howard felt as though his life up to that moment had been obliterated. It seemed that human beings were never really in a cul-de-sac; they could break out some way or other.

The notice about safety belts and no smoking had come on; pressure in his ears made him aware that the plane was descending to Pearls Airport in Grenada. He took up the handbook on the island which he had found among Meg's things and opened it to see if there was a map on a large enough scale to show Chèvre Point.

'Monotonous miles and miles of sea and wind endlessly beating against . . .' The fly-leaves and end-papers of the book were covered in Meg's tiny but meticulously formed writing. The entries were brief and in a condensed form that did not always make immediate sense, but he could see it was a journal of her holiday in Grenada the year before. He glanced through it quickly, spotting several mentions of Nancy Douce's name and others that he had not heard before. Who were General Fédon, Larry Paton, Dickie Carew? That he knew so little of Meg's trip was an eloquent testimony to their lack of communication.

The entries had an eerie fascination for him. With a mixture of curiosity and sadness he read on from the beginning: '. . . each other. Mussel black storm clouds. We have crossed to Gander because of strong cross winds and this will make the flight to Barbados more than 5000 miles. Shall stay tonight at the Lu-Mar Inn, Pollard's Plantation, St Philip, Barbados, Quincy Adams will meet me tomorrow at Pearls. He drives a blue Triumph Spitfire. He says I shall be just in time for the Carnival on the Monday and Tuesday before Lent (Ash Wednesday) and that I shall hear the guns go off at Fort George predawn on the Monday morning – that is the "Jouvet", "Jour ouvert" or "day open". Carne=flesh. Vale=farewell. Feeling low and homesick – in a panic of loneliness . . .'

Howard got up from his seat after the plane had landed and joined the queue, edging along the gangway thinking of Meg doing exactly the same thing the previous year, lonely and homesick. What a hypocrite he was! Meg had not really changed over the years of their marriage – she had remained much the same as she had always been, but he had become bored with her, as he had become bored with his job, bored with their social life, and, above all, bored with himself. Instead of facing up to this he had put most of the blame on her. The lies he had told himself were endless. At odds with its environment, the wily subconscious was able to invoke an attitude of stupor towards the universe, holding it, as it were, at arm's length while it manufactured plausible pretexts and excuses.

If he was really honest for just one moment, would his undemanding love for Catherine Gurney stand up to scrutiny? Wasn't the buried truth that he wanted to possess her as he had taken Jill Lammas? And it was perhaps because of this lust disguised as love that Meg had gone in despair, in 'a panic of loneliness', to that Oxford Circus platform. Liar, hypocrite, he thought as he swung his case up on to the customs bench. This rare moment of candour made him feel strangely remote and detached, quite out of place in this gay holiday crowd.

'Mr Howard?' Nick Howard?' As he moved away from the Immigration desk, his hands encumbered with his case, passport, and Meg's book, he heard his name being called through the doorway and saw a tall Negro dressed in a white shirt and dark blue shorts shouting and waving both hands. 'I'm Quincy Adams. Man, this is nice. Good trip? My car's just outside.'

As they emerged after shaking hands into brilliant sunlight, Howard paused to remove his jacket; even the lightest weight one he owned was unbearable in this heat. Quincy Adams grinned. 'It gets to you, doesn't it? You know I'm always meeting people straight off winter flights from New York or London. Snow, freezing winds, then – whoosh into perhaps 90 degrees ... This is mine'. He pointed with pride at a crimson Sunbeam Tiger. 'The fastest car I've owned but don't worry, there won't be any burn-ups. The island roads aren't planned for speed. There are more than sixty-five bays in eighty miles of coast, so the track round it is strictly in and out, in and out.'

The car was parked in the shade and when they were sitting in it Adams turned to face Howard. 'Now this is the position, Nick. Pearls Airport is on the east of the island, above Grenville. If we were going straight to Ross Point where I've arranged for you to stay tonight, I'd drive across the mountains, show you the Grand Etang, and so on. But your house at Chèvre Point is on the south coast and if you're feeling up to it, not too tired, I plan to go there.' He turned round to pat a basket stowed behind his seat. 'I've got a little picnic here. Some cassava bread and guava tart. Fruit. And I thought we might light a fire on the beach, fry some jacks and melongene, that's a kind of egg-plant ... But perhaps the idea don't appeal?'

'It does indeed,' Howard replied quickly. Adams' good nature and openness were plain. If Howard had come to Grenada just to be sure he was dealing with an honest man, he could have got back into the plane. 'Perfect. You couldn't have planned anything I would like better.'

Adams gave a delightful smile but his rather fine eyes remained pensive. For a large man he moved with unusual lightness and grace, as though doing the opening steps of a dance. There was a gentle quality about him – it was not a homosexual's manner but a lack of that modicum of aggressiveness which Howard knew was in himself and most other men.

The car moved off with a bit of wheel-spin and a swirl of dust. Adams drove fast but expertly, showing good anticipation and judgement. He made an expansive gesture with his left hand: 'A picnic's nice but, man, tonight you'll really be eating. At the Ross Point Inn you get only the best West Indian food, all authentic. Callaloo, crab-backs, pigeon peas, scrambled lambie – that's conch meat chopped up, and everything there is rather special! By the way you must tell me if there's anything on the island you particularly want to see . . .' He broke off to flash a sideways glance at Howard. 'Nick, it's going to be Nick and Quincy, isn't it? I wanted to say how sad I was to hear about Meg. I mean, she came out here just to see me about this house but we were soon good friends . . .'

'I know, I know,' Howard said quickly. 'Well, I did think I'd like to call in to see Nancy Douce as she was a friend of Meg's, otherwise I'm in your hands. Anything you suggest.'

'No, I can't arrange for you to see Nancy, I'm afraid. Simply because she ain't here. She's still in Europe – London or Paris I think. Yep, last time I see Mrs Douce she said Nancy was in France. But that's some weeks ago. You know, I introduced Meg to Nancy and within a day they were like this, very close, going everywhere together. Nancy she's sweet and mighty persuasive and her hobbyhorses become yours before you know it. By the time Meg left here I think she knew as much about General Fédon as I do.'

'Fédon? I meant to ask you about him. I've only heard the name. Who is he?'

Adams grinned: 'He ain't no one now. He was a mulatto . . .' Adams shrugged his shoulders and wagged his head from side to side, disclaiming the description – 'who owned an estate called Belvedere in the middle of this island. In March 1795, he led an uprising against the British. Took fifty-one British prisoners and had forty-eight of them put to death, in the presence of his wife and daughters, striding about giving the order "Feu". By the March of the following year his rebels were in possession of the whole island except for St George's and a post at Calivigny. Then the British got reinforcements of eight hundred men and fighting began again. Fédon's men were driven from their strongholds in the mountains to Mount Quaco which Fédon called the "Camp de la Mort". A final assault drove most of them over the precipice there, but the mystery is that no one knows what happened to Fédon himself. His life ended in a blank and he became a legend – hero or monster, depends on which side you're on.'

'Which side are you on?'

Adams grinned again. 'I don't feel very strongly one way or the other. But, for Nancy, Fédon is strictly a hero, a martyr for his people. You see it's largely a question of this colour business. Now colour's not important here. I mean I'm black, my brother's coffee coloured, my aunt could pass for white, okay it don't matter in Grenada. But Nancy's very light and she did some travelling in America where it does count. There was an incident once, I understand, so . . .'

Howard was interested to hear about Nancy Douce but at the same time he was absorbing sights, sounds, and smells as the car sped along a narrow road following the coast-line, climbing, dipping, and turning constantly. There was bird-song all about them and a strong smell of spice : nutmeg, clove, cinnamon, pepper and ginger. The forest glittered with exotic flowers and shrubs : he recognized jasmine, oleander, wild cotton trees which Meg had described, hibiscus, bougainvillaea, and poinciana. Always mountains towered above them on his right hand; on his left there were provocative glimpses of paradisial coves.

Adams sucked his teeth thoughtfully for a moment. 'Don't get the wrong idea. Nancy may go to town sometimes on the colour bit but she's not a coloured bigot. She just does feel intensely about many things. She's very inquisitive and has dozens of interests. Anything odd or unusual will take her fancy.' He held his left hand in the air so that Howard could see a slight tremor. 'You see this shake? It's a family thing, doesn't worry me a scrap. But Nancy looked into it. Found out it's called "The Mad Hatter's syndrome", that dentists often suffer from it by inhaling mercury vapour when filling amalgams. That quite made her day. And of course I became the Mad Hatter.'

The road had left a shadowy complex of hibiscus, Mexican creeper and tree ferns, and the Tiger shot along a comparatively straight avenue between bright green sheaves of sugarcane. There was a pungent smell of molasses. Adams said: 'Well, this is it. The parish of St David, the only one in the island without a town. Perhaps I shouldn't say it as I'm trying to persuade you to sell but I like this part of the island about best of all. Of course the finest sand beach, Grand Anse, is over on the west coast and personally I wouldn't want to *live* anywhere except St George's. But here you have a perfect climate. Sea-breezes to cool you off and enough rain to keep everything green most of the year. Farther along the coast, the south-west tip, Point Saline, is dry and arid. Yep, you've got a good site all right but as you'll see the house is in bad shape. Wait another year or two and all you'll have is a building plot.'

'Yes, I remember that Meg said about the wood-work being attacked by some insects. Doesn't your prospective buyer mind about that?'

Adams stopped the car and rubbed his hands together glee-fully. 'Man, this client Levine is so bugged on your coral reef I don't think he knows there is any wood-work. Joe Levine, he's rented the place for six months and not one complaint yet about the water pump which is a brute and throws its driving-belt at least twice a day. Levine is back in the States right now but when he is here he's out there snorkelling all day, hardly ever surfaces. Here we are then. Chèvre Point. We'll have to walk up that track. The house is just over the hill.'

The rough track led them past a series of roofless old barn-like buildings with a tottering stone aqueduct leading to a very large water mill. Adams pointed to this. 'That's a sugar mill, dates from about 1790. Swarms with bats but you don't see much of them on the other side of the slope. Your house was named after the old estate here, Chantymell, corrupt French like so many other names on the island. From cantemerle, blackbird. Now birds are one thing you've got plenty of. Bananaquits, Grey Kingbirds, Ground Doves, Laughing Gulls. You only own an acre of grass but you also possess a custard apple tree, a very fine sapodilla, a few frangipani, and, down on your strip of beach, some palms and one manchineel. If you decide not to sell but to emigrate here, then just watch out for that manchineel. The fruit looks like crab-apples but the sap is poisonous. Don't stand under it in a shower. Apart from that and a few under-water hazards like sea-eggs and fire coral there's hardly anything to warn you about. These are the friendly tropics, it's not like being in South America ...'

Adams seemed to have got wound-up on a promotion spiel, forgetting Howard was not there to buy. They came to the bungalow which Howard had seen in photographs. It was even smaller than he had expected; an unprepossessing building, amateurishly constructed, partly of reddish wood. It looked neglected and badly in need of repairs.

With a wave towards the sea Adams called out 'Pleasure before business. That's a good old Grenadian motto. What say we have a swim before probing the decaying tooth. I mean, man, that's a house one ought to be pleased to sell, eh?'

As they descended the slope to the sea Howard thought that Quincy had rather overdone the attractions of the place. The grass was wild and rank; cacti, briars, and weeds were thriving as if anxious to assert a supremacy. On each side of the narrow inlet there was high ground covered in jungle, and to the right it thrust out in a dark peninsula he took it to be Chèvre Point.

Once they were on the beach Adams threw off his clothes impatiently to reveal white and blue striped bathing-trunks. His apparent relish for the sea seemed surprising for someone who must have daily opportunities for swimming. He produced snorkelling masks and flippers while Howard was changing, then sat wriggling his prehensile toes sensuously in the white sand saying: 'Do you know that moment in the Debussy opera *Pelléas et Mélisande* where Pelléas emerges from the subter-ranean cavern to the air of the sea and the scent of roses?'

Howard smiled. 'I know what you mean.' There was indeed

balm in the sea and the sea-wind. Levine the absent tenant was right to spend so much of his time on the coral reef for it was decidedly the main attraction at Chantymell.

Adams said: 'The reef's about sixty yards out. The tide is low now so first we swim then we'll have to kind of paddle a bit as you'll find the coral will be only two–three feet beneath the surface, then swim again off the edge into the deep water. We'll land on Chèvre Point. While we're out there I can illustrate another reason why I think now is a good time to sell.'

Swimming had been Howard's pastime for most of his life; in his youth he had swum for a club and it was the one sport he had kept up, but as soon as they dived into the sea he knew he had met his master in Adams who moved through the water effortlessly like a dolphin.

Clambering over the barely covered reef was a tricky business and Adams moved slowly, pointing out clusters of black sea-urchins some of which had spines ten or twelve inches long. 'Now watch out sharp for the sea-eggs and don't touch any yellow coloured coral,' he warned, bending down to pick up a ball of gelatine-like substance which he held in one palm, touching it gently with a finger so that Howard could see the hardly perceptible throbbing. 'Octopus foetus,' he said with a tiny sideways movement of his head expressing a wonder of Nature.

When they dived from the coral reef into fifteen fathoms of emerald-coloured water Howard found himself in a world of fantastic variety and richness that made his memories of Mediterranean underwater expeditions seem dull and barren. Indigo parrot fish, with teeth fused into bird-like beaks, fed all around them; minute fishes teemed in jewel-like clusters; mysterious shapes hovered in the blue-veined shadows; clusters of tiny eels shot up from burrows, appearing like slim rules, then parentheses and question-marks. Niggerheads, clumps of brain coral, turtle grass, tube sponges, sargassum weed, sea-fan lace, and polyps made up a dream-like landscape.

Adams shot along, propelled by short movements of his legs and a graceful reaching forward stroke with his arms as if he was grabbing handfuls of sea. He was obviously familiar with this particular stretch of reef, pausing to inspect a huge calcareous dome that was the colour at the heart of a fire with a rayed skeletal pattern, then reaching in among white coral polyps to extract a brittle starfish. Later he turned and waved to attract Howard's attention to a dangerous outcrop of elkhorn coral beneath them which branched upward in grey, ghost-like arms.

It was a long swim and when they had waded out on to the soft sand that bordered a short stretch of Chèvre Point Howard was glad to fling himself down and recover his breath. Adams said, 'Now tell me, Nick, doesn't that make you feel one hundred per cent? There's a Greek tag I'm told which translates as "The sea cleanses away all the ills of man" and I know exactly what it means. You see, business-wise this island is known for its frustrations. Little things go wrong pretty much all of the time. In fact it's so bad that people even get to boast about it, how long it took to get a faucet mended, etcetera. Sometimes it gets on top of me and that's exactly when I take to the depths.'

The white sand was covered with palm leaves, splitting canes, rubbishy looking fibres. Beyond the line of palms there were a few dwarfish trees, creepers, and then the headland rose up covered with what looked like impenetrable jungle. Adams grinned as he followed Howard's eyes. 'Don't worry. We're not making a long expedition through that. Five minutes will get us to the top and then we can see all we want.'

The sea on the other side of Chèvre Point was lagoon-like and rather unattractive. The headland protected it from the breezes that kept Chantymell fresh, and the heat was terrific. Sunlight glittered on the still surface of the sea so that it appeared like mercury. Sweat was running freely down Howard's body and he had to wave his arms continually to keep the flies off his face.

Swivelling his head from left to right Adams said 'Not much good swimming-wise but it's a perfect anchorage for yachts. And *voilà* your neighbouring house, the famous Bellerêve!'

Tucked away in the corner of the sheltered bay Howard could see part of a large, imposing house. It looked empty and was shuttered, presenting an eyeless face to the blazing sun.

'Now there is the other reason why you should take the opportunity to sell Chantymell to Joe Levine, the man who just don't care,' Adams explained. 'When your parents-in-law lived here Bellerêve was always maintained in fine style. Oddly enough there are very few large colonial houses left on this island and that's one of the best. It's owned by the film star Jessica Dessart. Used to be quite a tourist attraction just to say that she lived here part of the year. But recently its reputation took a dive and Miss Dessart doesn't come here any more. It's shut up and without anyone going in to look after it likely to go to ruin I should say. But the important thing from your point of view is that it's got a bad reputation. People round here just don't like the place . . .' Adams gave an unhappy grin.

'What happened then – why don't they?' Howard had been trying to place Jessica Dessart whose name was a familiar one to him, as many other actresses of the 1930s, but could not at first remember a single one of her films. Then a scene from a silent picture she had made with John Gilbert, which he had seen in a revival, was slotted into the forefront of his memory: a touching little appearance in a melodrama of World War I where her great dark eyes and insouciant charm carried her successfully through a trite story.

'Well, it was always a great place for parties. Jessica Dessart spent money like it was going out of fashion. The bay would fill up with yachts – lots of big names – the fast set from Barbados – wild goings-on were run of the mill here. Strange tales sometimes. But last June there was a very unpleasant story about a girl – not the usual brango. This girl was supposed to have been dosed up with Spanish Fly. It's reputed to be an aphrodisiac. Concocted from the crushed wings of a beetle, called *lytta vesicatoria*, a doctor friend informed me. The aphrodisiac effect is dubious but it's dangerous stuff, sans doubt. *Officially* nothing happened – at least I never heard of any police inquiry. What is definite is that Jessica Dessart pulled out and they shut up shop at Bellerêve. Usually when she was away in Europe the place was kept immaculate – four or five staff here always. This time it was just locked up and left, period. It's a remote spot and there's a cemetery in the grounds, as in most of the big estates here. Now there are these local stories about jumbies – you know, ghosts.'

Howard stared again at the white shuttered house that grimaced in the sun like a blind man, threatened on three sides by the encroaching jungle. The stillness and silence surrounding Belle-rêve did seem rather sinister. At night in this deserted place one might readily believe in demons and not in the Father Christmas Christian God that belonged to rose-clustered English rectories.

'Let's get back to Chantymell, says I. I want to make a beach fire and cook those jacks. Yes,' Adams turned round, opening his eyes wide in mock terror, 'there's a strange satisfaction in lighting a fire like that. To start tigers of flame running riot in the twigs and straw. Aha!' He grinned. 'Now you can see I'm as much of a nut as those folk who say they've seen jumbies here. But seriously we've been lucky to find good old Joe who only believes in what he sees out on the reef. The story's not going to be allowed to die for quite a while if I'm any judge.'

5

Perched on an eyrie-like vantage point Howard and Quincy Adams looked down at the night scene of St George's. They stood on a very small stone parapet, fronted with railings, jutting out from the hillside, and had a panoramic view. Houses in the old town seemed to have found their own level and most of the lights were dotted about higgledy piggledy instead of being in rows, while others appeared to be suspended in mid-air and some danced slowly up and down on the sea. Everything had taken on a mysterious appearance in the still, warm night – the few clouds were motionless and unusually high, the rapt silence was one of suspense, as if the sky and earth were waiting for some esoteric ceremony to commence.

After a shower at the Ross Point Inn Howard had dined there with Adams on crab backs, chicken curry, and orange cream. No mention had been made of Mrs Adams and Howard was beginning to wonder if Meg had in fact said that she had met her. If she did exist Howard thought it was odd that there was no suggestion of meeting her. He had glanced through Meg's notes in the guidebook while he was dressing after his shower, but had not come across any mention of Mrs Adams though the narrative was peppered with Quincy's name and those of Nancy Douce and Dickie Carew.

Adams hummed a hymn tune and waved a hand about as if he was conducting a choir, then made a broad gesture to encompass the magnificent night sky. 'All this,' he said with a significant shake of his head, 'makes me think of "The day thou gavest Lord is ended" and once again I'm walking hand in hand with mammy and daddy to a prayer meeting with Mr Campaspe and Sam Douce, and ole Charley White is standing up telling about each and every one of us meetin' up again in heaven. Sam Douce, that was Nancy's father, was a very fine lay preacher. Died three years ago. Don't suppose I'll ever hear anyone like him. Always simple his little talks but they sure got to you. I remember him saying that faith was like taking a step in the dark and putting out a hand. I like that step in the dark idea. Fact is, coming here is killing two birds with one stone for you've got the best view bar none of St George's – and those steps down there lead to the Douce house. I thought you could pop down and make your call, then perhaps we could go on to a bar, have a rum punch or two, and look up one of Nancy's friends – Dickie Carew. He's quite a character.' There was a note of criticism or reservation in the tone of this description, and it was the first time that Adams had been anything but amiable.

'Ah yes,' Howard said. 'I think I've heard of Mr Carew. I'd like to meet him if you can arrange it.'

'Oh, we should be able to track him down. This time of night – Bar Bizarre or the Escapade I should say. He's rather predictable – like Joe Levine. The Carew family are big money and Dickie's never worked. He wanted something – his mother bought it for him. He's got one of the finest yachts in the Caribbean, *The Hesperides*. Meg and Nancy went out in it once or twice I think. Rather an odd-ball, Dickie, kind of moody and he comes in for a lot of criticism. Someone I know called him "a neurasthenic idler". But I don't doubt you'll find him interesting and on a good night he can be fun.'

'Fine,' Howard said, moving towards the steps. 'I shan't be long. Just want to clear up this business about the letters that were sent to our house for Nancy. See you soon.'

As Howard descended he felt like a blind man having to rely on the rail he gripped because the moonlight was obscured by overhanging trees so that when he heard rushing water he could not see its source. When he emerged from the tunnel of branches he saw a small waterfall and found a house sited on a narrow terrace that had been hacked out from the hillside. The position and view were magnificent. The house was a two-storied white wood building with a veranda running round three sides. The lush garden resounded with the noise of tumbling water, crickets and frogs. A young girl was descending the steps, moving rhythmically to music from a transistor radio which she held in one hand.

'Miss Douce? Nancy? I'm Nicholas Howard – Meg's husband.'

The girl stared at him nonplussed for a moment, then said, 'Miss Nancy not here. She gone. Comess. I don't know – you want to see her mother, Mrs Douce?'

Howard smiled and said yes. The girl continued to stare at him with a look that was at once inquisitive, puzzled and slightly coquettish. Her hair curled like watch-springs and her black eyes were so big and round that she looked just like a coloured doll that Howard's daughter had treasured for years. Suddenly she grinned widely and went back up the stairs, wriggling her hips in an exaggerated way in time to the calypso version of the Beatles' tune *She loves you, yeah, yeah* coming from her radio. At the top of the steps she turned to give Howard a bold, provocative look, then called out loudly: 'You come right on in, sir. I 'spect Mrs Douce see you in a little while again.'

The living-room was largely open to the veranda as the main windows had shutters but were not glazed. Two standard-lamps in the room and lanterns on the veranda contrived the pleasant effect of pools of light and shade. The walls were white with wooden lattice-work at the top and the outside doors had movable narrow wood louvres. There were several bowls of flowers. Looking round at the moonlit sea-view framed by the tops of immortelles, Howard thought that he had never seen such a delightful house and wondered why anyone should want to leave it to live in London or Paris. The girl had turned off her radio as she went upstairs, and in the silence Howard could now hear somewhere at the back of the house on the ground floor the occasional scrape of a knife and fork on a plate as if an invalid was picking at a meal. Then above him he heard a smothered exclamation and quick footsteps on a wooden floor. He turned towards the stairs as a woman appeared there holding out her hand.

'Mr Howard – you've seen Nancy?' Mrs Douce was of medium height and slim build, dressed in an immaculate white blouse and mustard-coloured skirt. Like Quincy's aunt she 'could pass for white'. Her coarse lustrous black hair was drawn back in a bun. She had a smooth nun-like forehead but her eyes were troubled.

'No – I was hoping I'd find her here. Actually I've never met her, but my wife ...' He broke off on seeing Mrs Douce's expression had become distracted. She dropped her hands in a gesture of despair, then shook her head saying: 'Oh, that silly girl Lucille. Oh dear, I thought – I hoped – you might have a message from Nancy. No, that's not fair – it wasn't Lucille's fault – I didn't give her a chance to explain. That's what we humans do when we're frightened.' She held her forehead as if to still some ache but her expression was calmer. 'Mr Howard.' She shook her head. 'You must forgive me. It's unforgivable inflicting this on you, but I'm so worried. Nearly out of my mind. I don't know where Nancy is and I've no idea what to do. Why she hasn't written ...'

'How long is it? Since you last heard from her.'

Mrs Douce could not answer straight away. She turned to hide her face, struggling with her emotions. When she did speak she was suppressing tears and she gulped so that some of her words were swallowed. 'Two months – it arrived – Christmas – France – upstairs – I was sitting there.' Howard was touched and wanted to help but he felt like an intruder, useless and somehow clumsy and loutish.

Mrs Douce beckoned him without another word, and he followed her upstairs and along a narrow passage to a small bedroom with a large window which gave it the illusion of being poised directly over the moon-blanched sea. They stood looking out of the window in silence and Howard felt that a bond of unspoken affection had sprung up between them. When she faced him her voice was under control. 'Excuse me a minute. I'm so sorry to be like this. I'll feel better in a few moments and then we'll talk. This is Nancy's room.' When she went out of the door an atmosphere of goodness, an invincible gentleness lingered on behind her like perfume in an alabaster vase.

The room was furnished with extreme simplicity and contrasted vividly with his memory of Jill Lammas's. The bedspread and rugs were white and there were white bookshelves beneath the large window. There was an old-fashioned wardrobe and chest of drawers of rather fine red wood. Howard's eyes were drawn to the only photograph in the room. It showed a slightly younger version of Mrs Douce and he presumed her two companions were her husband Sam, whom Quincy had said had died three years previously, and Nancy. Howard took the photograph and studied it closely under the light from the bedside lamp. Mr and Mrs Douce were holding Nancy's hands and all three were poised as if they had just given her a swing through the air. She was landing slightly in front of them with long thin legs spread out before her. They were all laughing. In the background there was the waterfall and the steep stone steps that led down to this house. Howard was struck by the quintessential oddity of this world, in which negative and paper preserved such a moment of simple happiness while the people concerned journeyed on to other things. He was remembering similar incidents with his own family when Jacqueline had been young, continuing to stare at the photograph which suddenly seemed poignant and fateful, seeing, as if in a magic mirror, the whole drama of human beings brought briefly together to love and be happy only to be parted for eternity.

A selection of Christina Rossetti's poems lay open on the bedside table and the poem on page 210 had been marked with a tiny pencilled tick. It was titled *One foot on sea, and one on shore*:

> Oh tell me once and tell me twice
>   And tell me thrice to make it plain,
> When we who part this weary day,
>   When we who part shall meet again.

When windflowers blossom on the sea
  And fishes skim along the plain,
Then we who part this weary day,
  Then you and I shall meet again.

Yet tell me once before we part,
  Why need we part who part in pain?
If flowers must blossom on the sea,
  Why, we shall never meet again.

My cheeks are paler than a rose,
  My tears are salter than the main,
My heart is like a lump of ice
  If we must never meet again.

Oh weep or laugh, but let me be,
  And live or die, for all's in vain;
For life's in vain since we must part,
  And parting must not meet again

Till windflowers blossom on the sea
  And fishes skim along the plain;
Pale rose of roses, let me be, –
  Your breaking heart breaks mine again.

'Life, Mr Howard.' He turned round to see Mrs Douce regarding him with moist eyes from the doorway. Her glance
went to the photograph and then the poem. 'It's funny.' Her
hands demonstrated an oblong shape, then fell limply to her
sides. 'Life slips through your hands and you don't really value
it while it's good. How difficult it is to appreciate what you have
when you've got it. Then it is gone, and nothing will bring it
back.'

'Perhaps I can help – about Nancy.' Howard could see that
Mrs Douce was still shaky and he took her hand for a moment.
'Let's sit down. You tell me about her.'

'Sam, my husband, he used to say it was possible to be happy
in the face of danger, serene in a storm. I know just what he
meant and it worked for him. You see he died after a long
illness, angina. He was in bad pain at times yet he was serene.
But I'm not like that, not at all. I've never got used to losing

him and now this mystery about Nancy. I'm frightened and . . . Still, I feel I shouldn't be inflicting this on you. Quincy told me about your wife . . . And of course I know I may have worked myself up into a state over nothing. A letter could come tomorrow and all this anxiety would be gone. You see Nancy doesn't write often. A few weeks go by and then I get one that's more like a book, ten, perhaps twelve pages, giving me all her news.'

'You had the last letter at Christmas?'

'Yes, she wrote it on the 14th December but even our air-mail post is not so good nowadays. Some people have lost quite a few letters, others get misdirected. And in that letter she said she was rather tired of London and might go to Paris for a while. Then a present she had sent, a cardigan, arrived at the end of December. I did try to see when it had been posted but couldn't make out the postmark, it was too blurred. Nothing since. And I've written three times to her address in Earls Court . . .'

'Bina Gardens?' Howard queried, and then continued when Mrs Douce nodded: 'Oddly enough I've been to that house. Some letters for Nancy were sent on to me – care of Meg actually – so I went round there. The landlord, Mr Patterson, a funny little nervous man, told me that Nancy had left and he apparently presumed she was coming to our house in Henley. I expect you know there was a suggestion of her doing that earlier on when she first came to Britain. October, wasn't it?'

'Yes. After your wife stayed here Nancy was very keen to stay in Henley. But then she got this job with an agency that supplied temporary secretaries and she had to be right on the spot. I haven't got the telephone number of her place . . .'

'Have you written to the police, Mrs Douce?'

'No. I've kept putting it off. I made the excuse to myself that I didn't know if she was in London or Paris, but really I couldn't bring myself to do it. In fact I told a good friend, Mr Campaspe, that I had because he went on at me, but I haven't.'

'Well, I may be able to help then.' Howard experienced a feeling of relief in realizing there was something he could do. A good deal of his professional life as a dealer in rare books was spent in tracking down leads, and he knew it was something he did well. He had been accused of being thick-skinned and over persistent in following up information. This looked like a situation where this fault could become a virtue. 'I'll go back to Bina Gardens – I'm leaving for England the day after tomorrow – and this time I'll get some definite information, I promise. Exactly when Nancy left there – why they were vague about her next address and so on. Quincy Adams is waiting for me at the top of the steps so I can't stay too long now, but I'll come back tomorrow and in the meantime you can write a brief note saying you want me to make inquiries on your behalf. Then, if necessary, I'll go to the police for you – do anything I can . . .'

'Really? That's very kind – but won't it take up too much of your time?'

Howard shook her hand and smiled. 'Not all that much – anyway I want to help. I mean that.'

As Howard went back past the waterfall and up the dark steps he was trying to marshal vague memories of what action the police took regarding missing persons. This rather pointless mental activity of recalling doubtful information about a Register and Bureau of Missing Persons was obliterated when he reached the stone parapet by a vivid mental image. In his mind's eye he saw a cliff-top scene in Pembrokeshire, a part of Wales which he and Meg had explored on their first holiday together. There was the curve of the remote cliff where they had seen goldfinches on a thistle-grove and a raven soaring above them. This was the scene of a lyrical but uneventful dream which had recurred often since Meg's death as if to summon him back, as if it had a message for him which he had not understood. It was an odd and disturbing experience to have it flash on his mind, looking real enough to step into, as he climbed a dark hillside in Grenada.

'What news of Nancy?' Quincy Adams' tall figure was half in, half out of his Tiger, awkwardly placed as if he had been adjusting something under the dashboard.

'No news I'm afraid. Mrs Douce is very worried because she hasn't heard from her since Christmas. Nancy wrote to say she might be going to Paris but not a word afterwards to say she'd arrived. I said I would make some inquiries when I get back to England. I'm not sure what I can do but I'll try.'

'Ah, so you too have fallen under the spell of the well-known Nina Douce charm! They've both got it. And Sam was like that too. Quiet, rather reserved, but there's something about them that gets you. Funny though, that about Nancy – it's out of character. She's a great one for going places, she was always singing that song *Trains and boats and planes*, but I can't understand her doing anything to worry her mother.'

Quincy was quiet for a while as he drove down towards St George's. When he did speak it was in a rather lifeless voice at first, as though his thoughts were elsewhere. He gestured backwards with his thumb: 'I was going to show you some other elegant houses in St Paul's, and then go along the Morne Jaloux road past Fort Frederick, a kind of razorback ridge to Woodlands, where you get a fabulous view. But if you don't mind we'll skip that now and concentrate on trying to find Dickie. He'll be concerned about Nancy and believe me there aren't many who impinge on him. They've been close – well, for five or six years, since Nancy was about sixteen. No *amour* you understand, it's something different to that. They're rather similar types.'

'You don't think she would have written to him and not to her mother?'

'Very doubtful, I'll allow, but just possible. I can imagine that happening if ... Well, anyway let's look him up. I was with the Douce family when Nancy first laid eyes on Dickie and vice versa. It was in Carriacou, that's a little island which we Grenadians look on as a holiday place. We were on the beach there at Hillsborough when Dickie brought his yacht in single-handed, anchored and swam ashore. He's a striking-looking fella, you know. He emerged from the sea looking like a Greek god, his hair bleached nearly white, came over to say hello to me, spotted Nancy and that was that.'

6

Quincy Adams parked the Sunbeam Tiger outside his Carib Estates office facing the dark and mirrory harbour. A party was apparently being held on one of the larger yachts which was brilliantly lit and the air resounded with laughter and steel band music. As they walked in the direction of the Carenage where boats were beached for repairs, Quincy put his hand on Howard's shoulder and spoke confidentially.

'You know what's wrong with Dickie Carew? Only one thing really. Spoilt. It's as simple as that. Have you ever met anyone who seems to have everything and yet there's something wrong, somehow working *against* him? There was a portrait artist here about a year ago who rather fell for Dickie, persuaded him to sit for her. She talked to me about this feeling you get with him, said that "Nemesis awaits as certainly though intangibly as in the overture to *Don Giovanni*". I s'pose it's just the case of having too much too young. You see the Honourable Mrs C. gave him 250,000 Beewee dollars when he was twenty-one and he knows there's plenty more where that came from. Then, looking like one of the more glamorous film boys, he's always been chased by plenty of people – and I mean people, both sexes. Not surprising if it's gone to his head and mixed him up, left him without a goal.'

There was a definite note of jealousy in this that puzzled Howard. Quincy Adams was endowed with good looks and a perfect physique; his business appeared to be thriving and not too demanding. Why should he envy Carew so much that it became obvious when he talked about him?

A small electric sign intermittently advertised the location of the Bar Bizarre on a second floor in what looked like a warehouse. They went up one flight of dimly lit uncarpeted stairs and then met the jostling overspill from the crowded bar. It was possible to see into the smoky room, erratically lit by moving lights, but entry appeared difficult. Quincy shrugged his wide shoulders and turned round explaining: 'Always like this till the band starts to play, then quite a few people with normal hearing suddenly find they have to leave. Nothing for it but to burrow your way in. Once you've caught up with two or three rum punches you don't notice the crush. Stick close behind me. I know the drill.'

Howard did his best to follow Quincy's instructions but it was rather like trying to push into a resilient mattress. The crowd was gay, vocal, and demonstrative, seemingly composed entirely of people who were four or five drinks ahead of him.

After a few minutes he found himself bogged down against a wall still some distance from the bar. Mysteriously a rum punch appeared for him, pressed into his hand by a heavily built American whose chest hair looked like barbed wire beneath a nylon shirt. Howard gave up the struggle to follow Quincy, sipped his drink, and listened to the conversations going on around him, mentally filing unusual words like 'mamaguey' and 'lougarou'.

Doleful background music was provided by a taped medley played on piano, double bass and tenor sax. It was a mechanical, hollow performance made much worse by the tape being badly worn, hissing, and occasionally eliding phrases. One after another of Howard's favourite tunes were done to death, ground out so that they sounded empty and meaningless. It was like a public demonstration of their ephemeral quality and the doomed nature of feelings they had inspired years before. Memories of Sinatra's early bitter-sweet *bel canto* in *All or nothing at all*, Glen Miller's *Moonlight Serenade* on A F N, Rodgers & Hart's *Blue Moon*, Bob Eberly singing *Tangerine* which he had played over and over again in a Hamburg canteen in 1945. Howard imagined that the performance might be climaxed by a public announcement: 'Well, that's it folks. That was the kind of music Nicholas Howard and some of his contemporaries found romantic. Strictly nothing.' Suddenly he felt as dated and out-moded as a cinema organ.

'I think I've spotted him, Nick.' Saying this, Quincy handed Howard another glass around the barrier formed by the American in ludicrously long Bermuda shorts and transparent shirt. 'We'll kind of edge along this wall. We're both in and out of luck. The band is going to play. You'll soon see what I mean. But we shall be able to move about freely.'

The tape was suddenly switched off half-way through butchering *Night and Day* and replaced by a steel band that was deafeningly loud. The home-made drums were played with enormous verve and élan – the rhythm was irresistible and Howard thought it would be delightful to follow the band in the streets of St George's, but in a comparatively small room the noise became a test for the eardrums that threatened to go over the edge and leave one without normal hearing.

Quincy shouted: 'Yeah, that's Dickie. In the striped sweat-shirt. Hell, he's talking to Colonel Garnett.'

Howard looked along the wall to see someone in a blue and white striped T-shirt and bleached jeans sitting at one of the hemmed-in side tables, listening with an unsympathetic expression to a tall man who had crimpy hair and a face as dead as a flash-light photograph. When they got closer Howard heard the tall man say in a voice raised too loud against the steel drums for the effect he wanted: 'So I said to him, I mean what a bore, threatening me with this dreary little bottle of barbiturates . . .'

Carew nodded mechanically but showed that the cadaverous man did not have his attention by twisting in his seat to call out to someone escaping: 'Good show, that man. A palpable hit. Take that man's name!' A flaxen-haired girl put her arms round Carew's shoulders as she passed without saying a word. Carew threw back his head to see who had embraced him and called out: 'I adore you, sugar, cos you're sweet. Hurry back you all, y'hear now.'

Quincy had not exaggerated Carew's good looks. He had thick fair hair which had been crew cut and then left to grow straggly so that the curls on his neck were as long as those on the crown of his head. There was a humorous twist to his mouth and an amused look in his long green eyes. A white scar on his wide forehead emphasized the deepness of his tan. He grinned as soon as he spotted Adams, saying, 'Welcome, welcome. I say, you've a fateful devilish appearance tonight, Quincy. Frightening and dashing, as if you've just escaped the clutches of the damned. But perhaps it's only the band.'

The tall pale man with the carefully waved hair, dressed in immaculate white trousers, shantung shirt, foulard scarf, and a yacht-club blazer, gave Quincy and Howard a cold look and walked away.

Carew grinned again. 'Mr Narcissus he don't miss us. Loved him, hated her. You know I sometimes feel like asking old Garnett, "If you had your time all over again would you still fall in love with yourself?" Who's your friend, Quincy?'

Adams ignored the jokes which had amused Howard. He said soberly: 'Nick Howard. You remember Meg, Dickie?'

Carew's grin vanished. He got up and put out his hand to

shake Howard's. 'I do indeed. Meg – we got on well I think. I'm so sorry, Nick, that we have to meet like this . . .'

Howard nodded, said 'I'm glad to meet you' and meant it. He found Carew's looks and manner attractive and was again puzzled at the subtle but persistent way in which Quincy had underlined his faults.

Carew said: 'You two sit down. I'll kind of lean on the table for a bit. Being a habitué of this dump I'm used to it. Tell me, what do you think of Chantymell?'

'Well, it's a wonderful site and the reef is beautiful – I had the best swim I can remember – but I agree with Quincy. If I was going to live in Grenada it would have to be in or near St George's. I've just been to see Mrs Douce. Now I thought her house perfection.'

'Ah, that's what I say. How is Nina? I've been away on a charter . . .' Carew broke off as he caught Adams' look of disbelief. 'You are a devil Quincy! You never believe I do any work. But I did have a charter and it was a very pleasant and profitable one. I took four nice Americans to Martinique, Antigua, St Kitts – then they wanted to explore some of the smaller islands so I've been away for over a month.'

'You won't know then that Mrs Douce is very worried about Nancy? Not having heard from her, I mean.' As Howard asked this he noticed that Quincy was not paying attention to the conversation but was watching someone on the other side of the room with a brooding expression. 'No letter since Christmas when Nancy said she might be going to Paris. Mrs Douce had written three times to her London address . . .'

Carew looked shocked, as if he had been slapped across the face, then grimaced as if trying to digest this information. 'But that's fantastic. Absurd. Christmas? I had a card from Nancy then. What the hell's up with her? Must be something serious.' He extracted a handful of things from his hip pocket and threw them on the table. Car keys, a few crumpled Beewee dollar notes, and two postcards.

'Look, that's all I've heard from her in four months, just a few words. But why should she stop writing to Nina?' Carew passed the coloured cards to Howard. One was postmarked from Ashkelton, dated the previous September, showing a

Roman Burial Cave; the other was a reproduction of William Dyce's painting *Pegwell Bay*.

'Have a look at the Christmas one. It's not private.' Carew straightened up, shaking his head from side to side. He said 'Well that's how it is' in a rather weary voice, then added, 'I'll get some drinks.' He rubbed his face, hesitated as if he was going to say something, then walked away. On the back of the Dyce painting Howard read 'Love and fondest Christmas wishes to Dickie from his girl Nancy'. The postmark was London 12th December and it was addressed to Carew care of the Spice Island Hotel. Quincy was now absorbed in watching Carew's slow progress across the dance floor and then appeared to notice some incident at the bar with a look of sly satisfaction. He muttered something in a scathing tone about 'Charisma'.

Howard put down the card and wondered if he hadn't had too much to drink. His head ached slightly but that might be due to the over-loud band. It had been a long day and the impressions he had gathered were becoming mixed-up. They were overlaid with the knowledge that Meg had experienced them a year ago. A momentary gap in the crowd allowed him an oblique view of the moonlit Caribbean. Meg had probably danced or sat in this room, spied those mast-lights bobbing up and down in the harbour, even heard that same tape – one of the tunes, *Moonglow*, was a particular favourite of hers. Following on in her footsteps was a curious experience – sometimes he felt that an extra mental effort on his part would reveal her reactions to these people and places.

'Fact is, Nancy took a terrible blow when her father died.' Quincy had picked up the pink-tinted card from Ashkelton and was studying the engravings on the rounded end-wall of the burial cave as if they might hold some obscure clue to Nancy's subsequent behaviour. 'But she bottled up her feelings because of her mother's. You saw that gash on Dickie's forehead. I say we all end up with scars, inside or out. For Nancy her father dying while he was still a comparatively young man, the pain he endured – I'm sure that scarred her. Left her restless, dissatisfied with life here.' He looked round arrogantly at the pleasure-bent crowd. 'She never put it into words but I could *feel* that she was saying, "What's the point of it all?"'

Dickie Carew approached in samba time holding the glasses high above his head. He moved with an insidious grace and for a moment appeared a Pan-like creature. He spoilt this impression by talking in a loud but slightly blurred voice: 'By God I've been trying to think of an explanation ...' He had a bit of trouble with the last word and paused like a stage drunk. 'But got nowhere. So frustrating. All right, a letter might have gone astray. I've lost a few myself. Okay, so then surely Nancy would have phoned. It's expensive and time-consuming we know but ...'

'I don't know about that, but Mrs Douce says she hasn't got a phone number for the place in Earls Court where Nancy was staying,' Howard explained. 'Immediately I get back I'm going to make some inquiries ... Mm – I've just remembered I shall have to ask Mrs Douce for a photograph.'

Carew raised his glass and called out: 'Well, here's to some good news.' He sighed deeply. 'This business makes me realize that I acted like a miserable bastard with little Nancy. Something about the whole Douce family, I suppose. That Christian bit. It's hard to explain. They're all so ... I mean they've had that old paralysed aunt living with them for about fifteen years, tying them down, but never any hint of complaint. And everything being for the best in the best of all possible worlds – that kind of propaganda. So I just had to stick a few pins in, chiselling away at Nancy's ideas.' He had a gloomy expression.

'Come on, cheer up, Dickie.' Quincy's tone was friendly now. 'If she was in hospital, had an accident, something like that, then surely Nina would have heard. Has it struck you – there's a possibility – well, I suppose it could be that Nancy has a reason for staying incommunicado.'

Carew laughed. 'To sum up. You are a character Quincy! All this subtle parlance. You mean she might be pregnant.'

'That or some other personal problem. It's *possible*.'

Carew gave this a moment's thought but shook his head. 'No, I don't think so. Anything – she could tell Nina anything. No, Nancy certainly left here looking for something, but it wasn't a fella. She was off on a quest for the Grail! The central human idea, Satori in Zen, moksha in Hinduism. "The truth behind the appearance of things." God, I remember saying I found something exciting about the idea of an aimless universe, in it all being a colossal pointless joke. If I do then why the hell don't I keep it to myself? And I kindly passed on to her that quote from Julian Huxley – "Operationally God is beginning to resemble not a ruler but the last fading smile of a cosmic Cheshire Cat". Yes, there's no doubt I said some mighty clever things. Just the stuff to cheer up a young girl who's mixed up and feeling a bit lost.'

Howard noticed that Quincy Adams was shooting odd frightened glances at Carew, rather as though he was a fizzing firework that threatened to go off at any moment. There was also something apprehensive in his tensed-up posture. Having spent an enjoyable day in Quincy's company, Howard was mystified at the effect Carew had on Quincy, like a catalyst changing his pleasant open personality into one that was subtle and slightly neurotic.

The three men had relapsed into an awkward silence. Howard was tapping his foot mindlessly to the rhythm of the steel band. He felt that, not knowing Nancy, he could not make a useful contribution to a discussion about what she might have done. Quincy was shifting awkwardly in his seat and looked decidedly nervous. An exotic girl was approaching them through the crowd, coming up behind Dickie purposefully as if she wanted to surprise him. There was plainly some Chinese blood in her which accounted for the complexion and the blue-black straight hair, so coarse that it could have been a mane on a rocking-horse, but she had eyes that looked as if they should belong to someone else, of deepest pansy blue. Her eyebrows appeared to have been shaved and were composed of tiny glittering hairs of uniform length. Her rather taut face lacked expression though there was wilful mischief in her eyes. She wore a sea-green dress cut low to expose the tops of her small breasts. She slid her thin hands over Dickie's eyes then gripped his biceps, tugging so that he slid from his half-seated posture on the table. He seemed to know who was holding him without looking at her, and partly resented it. He had an odd, embarrassed expression and said nothing. She continued to hide behind him as he came to his feet, then leaned forward impassively to whisper something in his ear. For a moment he seemed undecided what to do, turning to her reluctantly. Her arms went around his neck and they moved off into the slowly moving crowd of dancers. The girl called out 'Ciao' and Carew's expression became even more shame-faced.

Quincy sniffed and rubbed his chin. He nodded, eloquently expressing acceptance of something inevitable. 'There! You see, Nick! You remember that bit in *Westward Ho!*, "He learns me to be a toad!"?' Then seeing Howard's puzzled look: 'Oh I forgot. Of course you hadn't met my wife. Well, that's her – with Dickie Carew.'

7

Nicholas Howard stood at the door of his bookshop in New Cavendish Street fiddling with the key, uncertain whether the old Ingersoll lock had finally rebelled or his numb fingers were incapable of performing the simple action that was required. The snow that had covered the street when he left England had vanished without a trace, but there was a bitter north-east wind which cut through him and whistled round the corner of Westmoreland Street.

Returning from the West Indies to London on a Sunday evening in winter, particularly when it was done alone to open up an empty shop and flat, was like having an injection of undiluted midwinter cafard. Howard gave the key another irritated twist and the lock clicked open; he scooped up some letters and a note left on his desk by his assistant Harold Evans, then went quickly up the iron spiral staircase leading to his living room. Once he had closed the trap-door he began to feel warmer even before he had turned on any heating.

He opened his case and fished around in the confusion he had somehow contrived with only a few things; took out the bottle of Barbados Mount Gay rum and poured quite a lot into a tumbler. It was one of those evenings when it was easy to see how some people took to drink.

Howard was the temporary possessor of a telephone answering machine. Living alone above his business premises, he had thought it would be a good idea to have a machine that would record the names of callers and brief messages when he was out. The salesman of the it's-all-plain-sailing-just-sign-here variety had reluctantly demonstrated it rather as if he was a magician called on to do a difficult trick he did not wish to repeat. It had a number of disadvantages, the chief one being its effect on callers. After hearing the slightly eerie recorded voice saying 'You are being answered by a telephone answering machine. Mr Nicholas Howard is out but will be returning shortly. If you wish to leave a message please speak now ...' few of them seemed able to think of their reasons for phoning and some even forgot their own names. One of Howard's bookseller friends had told him that he felt completely intimidated by the machine and could never bring himself to speak to it at all.

While Howard busied himself in drawing curtains, lighting the gas-fire and bringing in an electric radiator from his bedroom, he gave the machine a glance from time to time. He had cursed the thing on several occasions, particularly when, returning late at night, he had forgotten to switch it off so that he had to race to the telephone in the morning and shout down it to the caller while the monotonous voice stated that he was out; nevertheless it did have a certain fascination. It was rather like having a fishing-net or lobster-pot waiting to be pulled up. Most likely there would only be the usual harvest of stammered names, maniacal laughter, slightly grating silences, flippant and obscene messages, but there might be some delightful surprise. There was no letter from Catherine Gurney among those he had collected downstairs, but it was possible that she had phoned while he was away. It was rather pleasant to circle the machine and imagine Catherine's voice outlining some unthought-of-solution to the dilemma they faced.

Making love to Jill Lammas, his stay in Grenada, and the Dickie Carew/Mrs Quincy Adams set-up, had all contributed to his decision that the 'affair' with Catherine should be ended, but nearly every way he had thought of doing this sounded presumptuous. He could simply admit to her, 'Look, is it worth risking your marriage to hold hands with someone who beds down with the first girl who gives him any encouragement?' but he dreaded doing this. Until he had heard the tape, the chance of an abracadabra remained.

When he did settle down to listening to the machine, poised with pencil in case there was something to be noted, there was the inevitable anti-climax. The tape did not include the wished-for call from Catherine; nor had Jill Lammas bothered to phone. There were the predictable names of a few business acquaintances; there was also the bogus offer of 'Lord Mellish's library' in a voice that sounded like Jake Wells doing his W. C. Fields imitation, and a rude request from an irate youth who had dialled the wrong number, pressed button A in error, and lost his money only to hear the machine's urbane announcement.

Right at the end of the tape there was an enigmatic message. After some heavy breathing an elderly voice began: 'Oh dear. Most trying. Is that *the* Nicholas Howard? Miss Voysey speaking. Edith. I can't leave a number. Oh dear, so inconvenient. Must speak to you. Miss Voysey. E ...' Then there was a noise as if the telephone receiver had been dropped and banged against something, followed by the unshaken, mechanically polite 'Thank you. Your message has been recorded.'

Howard wrote the name Edith Voysey at the bottom of the list he had scribbled, then doodled a question-mark and a big arrow. His interest in bookselling was at a low ebb and he did not feel inclined to see if a Miss Edith Voysey was listed in the London telephone directory. '*The* Nicholas Howard' was rather a laugh. If there was someone of that name of sufficient distinction to be so addressed it wasn't him, but he would wait until Miss Voysey phoned again to disillusion her.

Howard poured out some more rum and put Dvořák's E. major Serenade, the Deutsche Grammophon recording, on his record-player. The list of things he enjoyed was pitifully small: being with a woman he loved or liked, swimming in the sea, listening to music. But did he really envy someone like Toby Gurney who was interested in things as diverse as Wimbledon, fast cars, fireworks, Mensa and growing roses? On the other hand, with such a narrow range of interests and lacking a woman to love, his outlook was bleak. Once he had broken with Catherine Gurney he knew there would be no going back to the old status of family friend, and the love-making with Jill was undoubtedly the freakish result of a set of circumstances that would never occur again. He got up from his chair and fished in the case for the toy tiger with the realistically limp paws which he had bought at Pearls Airport in case he did see Jill again. He settled it on the arm of the couch with an odd feeling of regret for having got the thing.

Howard lay back in his chair listening to the Dvořák and brooding on his own psychological make-up. Somewhere he had read that 'all men as children are romantically in love with their mothers'. Was this obsessive longing of his for the perfect woman companion just some psychological hang-over from childhood which most men outgrew? Having no ambitions he was in the position that Curtis Mahon had described apropos Rossetti, finding in 'woman the embodiment of man's longing to escape from the triviality of daily life . . .'

How ironic that his one attempt to find a renewal of love had brought him so little but had led Meg to a critical moment of despair. He remembered the phrase 'in a panic of loneliness' in her notes on Grenada and tears came into his eyes. They continued to well up while he went to the window and stared up the street through parted curtains with a distorted vision that his eyes could not correct for a moment. The red traffic lights at the intersection with Wimpole Street shimmered, doubled. What a mess he had made of his life! That was probably the reason why he had fastened on the idea of finding Nancy Douce. He was sick of himself and wanted to escape by being involved in someone else's problems.

The ringing of his telephone brought him back from his futile brooding. When he picked up the receiver there was the same elderly, faintly querulous voice which the tape had last recorded.

'Is that Mr Howard? Are you really there this time? Mr Howard the bookseller who lived in Henley?'

'Yes – that's me. I say, I'm sorry about your other call – that machine business. If you had left a number I would have phoned back.'

'No – I couldn't do that. You see I'm telephoning from a call-box.'

Howard glanced down at his watch to see that it was ten-thirty, and wondered what matter could be so urgent to send Miss Voysey out into a bitter winter night.

'Now that I've decided... Made up my mind... I *must* see you...'

There was a long pause and Howard got the impression that his caller might be reading from notes. She continued hesitantly: 'So where can we meet? It will have to be somewhere near here as I can't be out too long. Because of mother.'

'Can you give me some idea why you want to see me, Miss Voysey? If it's about books, couldn't I call to see you at your house?'

'No – it has nothing to do with books.' Her tone was of barely controlled excitement, nervousness rather than irritation at being at cross purposes. Another pregnant pause. Then: 'It's about your wife – if it was your wife who died on the Underground just before Christmas?'

For an unpleasant moment Howard wondered if he might be dealing with some telephone crank, a ghoul who had read something into the report in the papers and decided to harry him. Perhaps all this vague chat was just the preliminary to an outburst of wild accusations. This time it was he who paused. So this was what she had meant by '*the* Nicholas Howard'. His acknowledgement was reluctant: 'Yes – she did.'

'Then it's quite vital I see you. Can you meet me in Highgate? About tea-time. I can get out while mother has her tea. But not tomorrow, the doctor comes then. Say Tuesday.'

'But where do you live, Miss Voysey?' To tie her down to an address seemed the best way of finding out if this might still be a cruel trick.

'Calvert's Hotel. Oh dear, I didn't mean to tell you that. You mustn't go there! I *forbid* it because of mother. Mother must *not* be involved! That's the crux of the matter. Look can you meet me – oh in Swains Lane, Highgate, at tea-time but before it gets dark. Say four o'clock. Just for a few minutes. I simply have to talk to you. But you must *not* come to the hotel!'

There was a note of genuine anxiety in her uncertain voice and the repetition that touched Howard. 'No, of course not. I wouldn't dream of it...' He had decided that a trip to the Archway would not take up much of his time even if it was on a wild goose chase. 'But where is Swains Lane? I mean is it long? Can we be sure of meeting there?'

'Near the cemetery gate. I shall be wearing a dark blue coat and hat. Good-bye.' The line went dead. Howard felt cold and empty even though the room was now at a reasonable temperature. He knew that he would not easily get to sleep with this mysterious business about Meg hanging over him. He took off his jacket and put on a thick fisherman's pullover. There was no food in the flat, but more rum would make him feel less empty and gradually help to blot out useless thoughts as to the significance of Miss Voysey's call. He was positive that Meg had never mentioned Edith Voysey's name. There was a list of names and telephone numbers in Meg's diary but that was in the locked-up house in Henley.

Howard took his clothes out of the suit-case and began to put them away just to have something to do. At the bottom, with his shoes and the box of assorted spices he had bought for his mother, the guide-book on Grenada containing Meg's notes about her trip lay open with one end-paper crumpled. He smoothed out the page and began to re-read the notes which he had previously skimmed through when looking for names and places.

Early on there was a list of shrubs and plants to be found in Grenada, apparently selected for their pleasant-sounding names, which for some odd reason reminded him of his recurring dream about Pembrokeshire so that once again he saw Meg standing on Nob Head looking out towards Skomer Island. He stared at the list until he remembered that Meg had once written down all the flowers they had found on the Pembroke cliffside: figwort, centaurea, camomile, foxgloves... She had often talked about that long-ago holiday, recalling the gold-finches flitting round their thistle-grove and the call of the stonechat on the brambles: 'Wheet, tick-tick'; but why should the brief idyll continue to haunt him? On a mental screen he pictured Meg and himself walking there, picnicking on the beach, making love; he examined images conjured up from the past as if under a magnifying-glass, but any deep significance still eluded him. With a mental shrug he returned to Meg's notes.

'Manchineel trees – juice of the bark or fruit blisters the skin (supposed to have nearly killed Nelson); "shack shack" alias woman's tongue with its clacking yellow tongue; Jerusalem thorns with lemon-coloured blooms; pink poui; elephant grass; black willow; seagrape.

'Half-ruined sugar-mill near Chantymell dating from the late eighteenth century. The mill now nearly surrounded by jungle but there is a tiny, isolated small-holding, hidden from the track, with a few geese and black pigs. The mill buildings swarm with bats. Quincy exchanged a few words with the small-holder about the Carnival: "What you jumping?" "Jump-up". Quincy told me about a quaint old private cemetery on the large estate "Bellerêve", near to Chantymell, which we may visit one day if he can contact the owner, Jessica Dessart, who was a film-star in the 1920s and 30s – her fame escapes me.

'9th February. Sailed in Dickie Carew's splendid yacht *The Hesperides*. Dickie really is an extraordinarily attractive young man. Thick curly fair hair which is bleached nearly white in places by being in the sea so much. Very casual and easy to get on with: happy-go-lucky and indolent unless something happens to take his interest. Nice smile. Reckless look in his eyes sometimes. Apparently he rarely refuses a dare and has broken a collar-bone, six ribs and punctured a lung in consequence of this. His green eyes take on the colours of the sea. Nancy Douce very much smitten; I suppose I might be if I were younger. Sailed from St George's past Grand Roy, Charlotte Town, and anchored in St Mark Bay to visit Victoria. Dickie rowed us ashore in a dinghy and then plunged into the sea to pull the boat in so that the white sand stuck on his legs like tinsel. Visited the Dougaldston Estate (one of the finest on the island) where they process nutmegs, mace, limes (lime oil), cloves, tonka beans. Nutmegs a very important product here. Nutmeg trees "mystica fragrans" – "male and female created he them". Trees grow two or three feet apart. The males flower first. Female trees are planted 20 to 30 feet apart and the male trees are planted between. When Dickie guilelessly recounted these simple facts about the nutmeg trees they took on a faintly stimulating sexual significance. True and at the same time absurd! A prolific tree can bear up to 5,000 nutmegs a year. Mace is the scarlet membrane or jacket of the nutmeg – when powdered it is used as a base for perfumes and cosmetics . . .'

There was a scream of brakes in the street outside Howard's flat followed by persistent honking, continuing so long that it seemed to demand attention. He went to the window and looked down. The source of the noise was a yellow Mini with something painted on its side in hectic colours. The car had stopped just below him but the honking continued for no reason he could see – there was no other car in sight. Then a female figure in a dark coat and hat got out and shook her fist at his window. There were two more derisive honks, and the car shot off in the direction of Marylebone High Street. Howard realized it was Jill Lammas gesturing at him.

When Howard got to the bottom of the spiral staircase he saw that Jill was banging with unmeasured blows on the glass door. She wore a very short black coat, white stockings, and a round hat, shaped like a pudding basin, decorated with silver stars, pulled down low for comic effect.

As he opened the door she stepped nimbly past him saying, 'Freezing.' She had a faintly amused expression. He turned round and leaned forward to kiss her cold cheek. There were so many scents about her that the effect was that of a pot-pourri, embalmed flowers contending with orris root and cinnamon bark. But also patchouli and somehow a whiff of the alien Carnaby Street world of fright-wig mops, Zapata moustaches, and Buffalo Bill characters with tobacco-plug curls, leather-fringed coats, and dirty ankles. Her face had been plastered with white powder and spangled with gold; her eyes were exotically made up with heavy black lines on the lids. She shivered and pulled away from his kiss, and his expression must have shown surprise for she said slightingly: 'Ooh look – it's gone all sulky!'

In among all the other odours there was the smell of whisky. Howard wondered if his encounters with Jill were going to be a reversal of those of Charlie Chaplin with the millionaire who when he was drunk liked Charlie but sober could not bear the sight of him. He said lamely: 'I was hoping you'd phone but this is much nicer.'

Jill gave him a disconcertingly blank look as if she had never seen him before, then said: 'Well, how it is. You see I was in this trattoria eating their so-called prawn cocktail and in it I spied something like a big snail with long horns and I'll swear it winked at me and I felt sick – so of course I thought of you.' She giggled. 'Actually it's the only time in my life I've acted with admirable tact – shown such consideration for others. Quick as a flash I whipped up my napkin and hid the beast. Then . . .' She teetered about a bit on her very high heels, giving the impression of a child who had put on her mother's shoes. 'Then I thought to the hell with them. I've done enough for them. Young boys, you see, darling! Quite hopelessly young, not my speed at all. All right, I thought, now I'll search out old monkey brand.' Howard raised his eyebrows in mute interrogation and she seized his right wrist, jerking it up and pointing at the hairs that showed at the end of his pullover sleeve: 'You see. Just like my old man. And mother called him monkey brand.'

Howard felt even older than her old man; much too old to keep up with this glib patter and the fencing that seemed to lie behind it. He stood still, not bothering to think of a quip, not caring if she was to spin on her heel and leave him. She began to walk round the darkened shop, lifting her feet very high and putting them down with exaggerated care in a theatrical effort to be quiet. She pointed at the bookshelves and said in a stage whisper, 'I say, are these all old books with the s's that look like f's? Then sucks to you, all you old books.'

She had obviously had quite a lot to drink – more than that Howard could not tell: he did not know if she was drunk, if she had wanted to be invited upstairs and stay for a while, or if she had come merely to make fun of him. Perhaps the memory of their uninhibited love-making rankled now; he might have to pay for it with some kind of emotional scene.

'Seriously, what do you do here? I mean apart from pretending to sell old books. Now don't tell me that isn't a front. Where does all the loot really come from? In this flash medical area, suitably adjacent to Harley Street, with all these windows full of surgical instruments – it makes you think. Is it a quiet line in abortion? Do say if it is as I have friends who have friends . . .'

Howard felt that there was a genuine probing of his financial status going on somewhat disguised by the frivolous questions. It was possible that was the only way he could keep her interested, by pretending to be wealthy, buying her expensive gifts, taking her to dine at Annabel's. He hastened to disillusion her: 'I've got very little loot. Just a reasonably large overdraft and a bank manager who broods on my deficiencies.'

'What about the old West Indies estate then?'

Howard laughed. With this frank question he felt completely at ease. 'Estate! That's good. It's a shabby bungalow. So small if you put some deck-chairs inside it would look like a tennis hut.'

She came close to him and had a strangely serious expression as she asked: 'What is this tennis business? My mother was always going on about the tennis bit. She made it sound so wonderful. Before the war. Tennis, long summer afternoons. Cucumber sandwiches and tea on the lawn and then sitting about in deck-chairs as the shadows grew longer. Yet no one seems to play it now, they just watch Wimbledon.'

Howard ignored this. He could not really believe she wanted to hear about tennis and he was rather tired of being placed in her parents' epoch. He pointed at the spiral staircase. 'Look, it's cold down here and I would have invited you upstairs where it's reasonably warm before this but I just can't tell what you want. I'll get you a taxi if you prefer.'

'Upstairs, you fool. Don't worry! It's your warm hands I want; not your cold heart.'

When the trap-door had been closed and concealed with a white rug kicked into place, Jill took off her hat and coat to reveal an equally brief dress of coral wool. She looked round with pleasure at the rather bare room, the couch covered with sage-coloured velvet, the two red leather armchairs, the white walls decorated with Samuel Palmer prints. 'But this is luxury indeed. Yes, methinks still there must be some sly scheme afoot whereby you get the loot to pay for it.' She took off her shoes and padded over to kneel on the couch and peer short-sightedly at the 'Bright Cloud' engraving of lovers on a hill-side.

'Would you like some coffee?' Howard asked. 'I only got back from Grenada a few hours ago, so like you the other evening I can't offer milk with it. Or there's rum.'

'Nothing to drink thank you. Oh yes, how was your trip to Grenada?'

'Interesting, enjoyable, financially worthwhile. I arranged to sell the tennis hut. Did some snorkelling and saw my first barracuda. Heard lots of steel bands. Drank too much rum. Incidentally I've got to make some inquiries about a Grenadian girl who came to London and now seems to have gone to ground. Do you have any idea whether the police would look for her? Or would they think at her age, she's about twenty . . .'

'I say I say, I do not wish to know that. What you really mean is was I ever in that position. No, cheeky, my parents went through the door marked nevermore and I'm on my tod. No they didn't. Oh I'm such a liar. It gets a habit! Stand still a moment darling and stop being nervous, offering me drinks and talking about Grenadian girls and stuff.'

Jill quickly moved close up to him, putting her arms round his neck, but he made no attempt to hold her. She smiled and her eyes moved up and down, up and down, from his mouth to his eyes. Catherine Gurney had done the same thing but with her Howard had felt it was an unconscious thing prompted by love. With Jill he was not sure whether it was a sign of affection or a stroke of artifice. She continually had him wrong-footed.

'You're alarmingly strong. I remembered the steel-type neck, but what's this great wedge of muscles between the shoulders?'

'Simple. I used to be a boxer. Many moons ago, but *not* when your mother was playing tennis. In the army at the end of the war. Now I swim a lot. To change the subject, did you see that tiger on the couch? He belongs to you. I've just been minding him.'

She ran to the couch and stroked the cub, looking quite life-like curled there, then picked it up and threw herself down backwards, showing lots of white covered thigh. 'Come on, I want to cuddle both of you at once. Or does that sound too decadent?'

8

'Twelfth February 1968. On board *The Hesperides* again with Nina and Nancy Douce, Quincy Adams, Larry Paton (who I'm told is a "friend" of the one-time film star Jessica Dessart – apparently this is his sole occupation) three Americans whose names I could not sort out from their nicknames, "Able"?, "Bubbles", "Casey", and the skipper Dickie Carew. Dickie quite different when he is sailing: a reassuringly capable personality emerges – he has crossed the Atlantic single-handed – was most impressed by this but he says it is quite commonly done nowadays.

'Dickie has made some inquiries about the chances of going to Bellerêve and they appear remote. Larry Paton says that Miss Dessart is becoming somewhat of a recluse but Dickie knows they still have the occasional party there, and then champagne flows like water. Larry said, "Jessica has aged terribly and can't bear strangers to see her face now that it's so lined". A pity as I was looking forward to inspecting Bellerêve at close quarters – it looks very grand from a distance.

'When we were at anchor in Morne Rogue Bay, near a one-time leper settlement, Dickie showed us his superb sea-shell collection, all very orderly with neat notes as to where rare specimens were found. He has a large number of sand dollars, or, rather, the white skeletons of sand dollars which are of the group Echinodermata, the same family as star-fishes and sea-urchins. Rarely seen alive as they live in deep water, but then they appear as if covered with green velvet. The skeletons relatively common, found in shallow water, resemble roughly circular shells. Pattern on top like an engraved star but this combines with six fissures to give the impression of a face. Curious, rather haunting things.

'Dickie (wearing his other hat, that of the knock-'em-down nihilist philosopher) picked one up and said: "I like this fella. Here we all are futilely trying to get to the heart of things and probably it's only a stone-dead heart of things, like the sand dollar". I think he says things like this just to provoke Nancy into opposition. Nancy and Nina are Christians with a simple, rather appealing faith; Sam Douce, Nancy's father, was a preacher here, still widely remembered for his favourite texts such as *"Duc in altum"* – "Launch out into the deep." Nancy's beliefs seem a bit wobbly under pressure, like mine. She's very restless, rather dissatisfied with this small closed community, hungry for ideas and knowledge of any kind. I suspect she's in love with Dickie Carew who refuses to take her seriously and treats her like a young sister.

'Nancy's enthusiasms are highly contagious and in a few days she has engendered in me an interest in (a) General Fédon who led a rebellion here in 1795 and disappeared mysteriously when it was quelled; (b) native semi-religious meetings something like seances – one that took place at Sauteurs was reported to Nancy as being accompanied by "Perfumes, whistlings, smell of burnt feathers, bursts of music, apparitions of strange birds, women in old fashioned clothes..."'

Howard had been reading more of Meg's notes on Grenada while he sat in the hall at Christie's waiting for a sale to finish. He had been singularly unsuccessful with his bids, which had all been in the first half of the auction, but had waited because he wanted to contact Alan Watson whom he had noticed sitting close to the auctioneer's dais. Hearing a stir upstairs which meant that the sale was concluded, Howard put the handbook on Grenada in his overcoat pocket and went out of the front door into King Street.

The sky was a delicate clear blue with a few snuff-coloured clouds moving rapidly away towards the west: a deceptive backcloth as it was extremely cold, much more bitter than when the sky had been filled with snow. Howard turned round and nodded at some of the dealers, who all emerged from Christie's looking slightly dazed and then were brought back to reality by the punishing east wind.

When Watson descended the steps he had his usual mocking smile as if to indicate that he did not take commercial ups and downs very seriously. 'Hello Nick. What a farce, eh!'

Howard said: 'I know. I didn't get a chance to open my mouth. Each lot started at about my mark.'

Watson took off his Glen Miller glasses and rubbed his

protuberant eyes. 'And to hell with Burgundy! Have you ever thought it would be rather nice, on a morning such as this, to throw a tantrum at a sale? Just to lie on the floor, kicking and shouting "Shan't! – won't – so there!"' It had been a sale so dominated by an 'Emperor' bookseller from New York that all the other dealers had wasted their morning.

Howard nodded. 'I know. By the way, talking of being out-classed, do you know how I might contact Henry Bailey? I phoned his office but his secretary said he was away and nothing more. Very cagey. I know he's a friend of yours. Is he abroad?'

Watson removed his glasses again and swung them judicially: without them he had an unscrupulous look. 'Don't tell me he owes you some cash and you want to suggest a method of dis-gorgement.'

Howard laughed. 'That will be the day. No, on the contrary, he did me a favour, a generous act. I'm grateful and want to say thanks, but not just in a note.'

Watson's look turned to disappointment as the chance of scandal receded. He shrugged. 'I heard a whisper he was staying in France, some château in the Dordogne. With one of those customers who is down to his last fifty million new francs.'

'God, where does he find 'em?' Howard asked. 'Frankly, that's the favour he did for me – put me in touch with a wealthy collector. I hardly ever contact one like that, let alone have so many that I can afford to pass them on ...'

Watson broke in by whistling the opening bars of the Eton Boating Song: 'Well, for one thing, he's got all the right kind of handicaps – Eton, Magdalen, that kind of thing. Where-as ...' He hunched his shoulders, sucked in his cheeks, and then spoke in a whining Cockney accent: 'You and me, guv, why we're always on the outside, just a-lookin' in. Admirin', envyin', oh oh oh sir! Never mind, Nick! Press on! Are you heading in the general direction of Charing Cross Road?'

'No, I must get back to my shop and have some lunch. Thanks, Alan. See you.' Howard waved and started to walk along to St James's Street. On the corner of Bury Street he heard hurried steps behind him and a heavy hand descended on his shoulder. He swung round to confront Jake Wells who said, 'So it's true! I heard you had emptied your piggy-bank and come to the big city. Well, you're playing with the big boys now!'

Jake was wearing an astrakhan hat at a rakish angle which suited his floridly handsome face. His heavy brown overcoat was unfashionably long and looked as if it might have been made up from a carpet, but was much more practical than Howard's in bitter weather. Whatever the season, Jake's clothes always had a faintly foreign appearance; he had a baroque personality which enabled him to carry off theatrical and eccentric garments. Ebullient, full of self-confidence, he accepted surprised looks from strangers as being his due. He clapped his hands together as if to draw attention to his black knitted gloves with a big hole in one finger tip.

Howard smiled. It was difficult to do business with Jake, or at least it was if one wanted to finish up with the illusion of having done well out of the deal, but his charm and gaiety were such that it was hard to resist becoming involved in his plans. He had tagged along behind Jake on many occasions and had rarely regretted doing so. He pointed at him and said: 'You old bastard. It was you, with the W. C. Fields' voice, who offered me "Lord Mellish's library" on the phone?'

Jake shook his head and did his Fields' imitation: 'Not a cha-ance, my boy. No sir, not a cha-ance.' Then he looked down mournfully. '*Nisayon Elohim.* God is testing me. Now my shoes are beginning to squeak.'

After looking round to see if anyone in St James's Street was interested in the problem of squeaking shoes, he moved off up towards Piccadilly, giving Howard a shove in the same direction. 'But piles I have yet to get,' he said in a thankful voice. 'Yes, it's a cheering refrain that. Try it as you walk along – piles I have yet to get – puts the bounce back into your step. Come on, Nick, join me in a plate of hot pastrami. Or salt beef yet. The Stage Door in Thayer Street. Just round the corner from your new premises.' He began to nod continuously, urging Howard's decision while making his eyes twirl round like Harpo Marx so that Howard laughed.

With a sideways leap Jake was in the road waving wildly at a taxi, acting out a great emergency. He jumped into it muttering,

77

'At last, my man. 22B Baker Street, cabby. No, make that Thayer Street and don't stop for the lights.'

Once he was certain the taxi was taking the quickest route, Jake turned round to regard Howard with a thoughtful expression in his slightly bloodshot dark brown eyes. 'Sorry I was away – and didn't write...' He gestured vaguely but Howard knew him well enough to understand that this blank was intended to encompass Meg's death. 'Not that letters help – you know ...' The sentence tailed off again. Jake was seldom stuck for words and this was a rare moment of embarrassment for him. Howard realized at that moment what a release it would have been for him to have had a friend with whom he could have discussed the events leading to Meg's death and his subsequent daunting sense of guilt. To have talked it over would have helped him to rationalize his position, but instead he had retreated farther and farther into himself and during nightmarish nights, after the inquest and the cremation, had formulated his cul-de-sac view of life. Now it was too late to attempt to unburden himself, and he could not have talked to Jake about such personal matters, but he did feel encouraged to speak of his vague plans for the future.

Jake was doggedly silent, as if forcing himself to remain quiet until Howard had said something. When Howard did speak he blurted out the sentences, running them together. 'I've made a complete break, I'm letting the shop in Henley, selling the house and my car, living over the shop in New Cavendish Street. My daughter's at the Sorbonne but there's a spare bedroom when she wants to stay with me ... It's rather strange at the moment but I expect it will work out eventually.'

'Of course it will.' The unusual diffidence had been replaced by Jake's customary note of confidence. 'Dealt all the rotten cards in the pack, you've just got to keep playing. Hold on. That's all anyone can do in bad times. How's business since you moved?'

'Not bad. I've got a very competent young assistant. My bank manager had me hamstrung for a while.' Saying this, Howard smiled inwardly at the strict rules of behaviour dictated by his sense of pride. Two weeks previously, when his financial position had been difficult, he would not have admitted this to anyone; but now that the prospective sale of Chantymell had been communicated to his bank he had left the period of money troubles behind, and it now looked like a molehill. 'During the time I was stretched, I was tempted by a rather curious deal. Do you feel like hearing about it? I could do with your sage opinion.'

'I know, I know.' Jake nodded. 'You regard me as being like Socrates' slave who worked out the *pons asinorum* with a stick in the sand. Flatterer!' He looked pleased at the direction the conversation was taking.

The taxi had stopped outside the Stage Door and Jake mimed his pleasure at seeing someone he knew at the back of the restaurant, then did a brief tap-dance as they entered. When they were seated Howard said, 'I'll keep it brief. Don't want to take up too much of your time with my problems.'

'Don't be a *schmock*. It's true I like to talk – but I can listen.'

'Ten days ago I had a phone call from Henry Bailey. A minor event in itself as it's the first time he's ever contacted me. To be honest I was rather pleased. He said he knew where there was a certain rare book, not in his own field, for sale at X pounds. He also knew a collector who was keen to buy it at X plus fifty. Mr A the collector wanted someone to negotiate the business so he could remain in the background. Bailey gave me some vague reason why he didn't want to handle it himself, also said it would be a good contact for me and guaranteed it would all be okay. I was a little suspicious, but on his say-so went through with it and the deal worked out just as he said it would. In fact I got an extra fifty as a retainer on the possibility that I might be wanted to act for Mr A in another transaction. So I was one hundred pounds in pocket, but I ended up with the feeling...'

'That you were just a pawn,' Jake suggested helpfully. He had a habit of finishing other people's sentences for them, not always accurately.

'Not exactly. Well, I suppose I did feel I was the man in the middle. It was as if I'd witnessed a conjuring trick without having it explained afterwards. Really I was puzzled. Why should Bailey ask *me*?'

'The answer's a lemon.' Jake paused. He was a raconteur in

the Jean Gabin tradition, fixing a listener with a glance at a strategic moment, waiting for reactions, judging his timing to a nicety, telling stories with obvious gusto. Howard envied him the gift, but lacking the facility did mean that he could concentrate on being a good listener, and there was a certain enjoyment in being like a camera and recording machine.

'You need advice?' Jake looked up to the ceiling in exaggerated astonishment. 'Presented with fifty quid for toddling from B to A and you need advice? You're like this young chap I know who keeps having it off with all these young birds and asks me what he should do about it. *I* should tell *him* what to do? Still I see what you mean. On the rare occasion that I've been offered a gift horse I've always looked at it rather carefully in the mouth. It's certainly rum. But then Bailey's not short of fifty quid, to put it mildly. And I can think of circumstances. What book was it, or is that a secret along with Mr A's identity?'

'A valuable erotic book. *Not* pornography. Rather lovely erotic plates.'

'Ah, that may well be your answer. Possibly Bailey's got a Nonconformist background or conscience that would not let him touch it.'

'Perhaps. Then why me? I've sold the odd volume of erotica but only a handful in as many years. I haven't got a reputation for dealing ...' Howard felt there was a whining tone creeping into his voice as he always did when embarked on a statement of self-justification. And after all, what did he know of his reputation in the book-trade?

'Why you? Because ...' Jake grinned. 'Because Bailey is a psychologist. You've got to admit he had you bang to rights ...' He broke off to order two plates of hot pastrami with cole-slaw salad, dill pickles, and beer. When the waitress had gone he continued, 'Yes, he judged you to a T. You want to hear the truth, Nick? I've always thought of you as a man, not a cypher. An individualist. A loner. That's the good part. Do you want the rest?'

Howard said, 'Certainly. After the Lord Mayor's parade comes the dustcart. I've had the compliments.'

Jake studied him closely to judge his reactions. 'Okay, well, if

I was pressed I should have said you might be willing to cut a few corners. And why not?' Jake went on to muse aloud: 'The motto of business? Why "anything goes", surely?'

'And just how have you gathered this impression?'

'That broken nose for one thing.'

'I'm sensitive about my nose.'

'All right, you won't settle for the jokey answer. That "ring" business then. Didn't you have trouble with the Antiquarian Booksellers' Association over that? There was some story, though I've forgotten the details.'

Howard bridled. It seemed to be his day for self-justification. 'The "ring" story. I went to a sale last winter in Wales. The day I got there a blizzard hit the Black Mountains area and we were practically marooned. Another bookseller and I got to the house on the view day and then couldn't leave that night. So we had to sleep there. The only other bookseller who came couldn't get through at all for the sale, and when we met up with him afterwards we re-sold some of the books to him. There wasn't a ring. There was no settlement.' It seemed as if he was going to be dogged by this 'ring' story. The interesting part of that sale was the night he had spent in the house that was to be auctioned, sleeping in musty blankets that the auctioneer's clerk found in a cupboard. He had rejected a damp bed and had drowsed fitfully on the bare floor downstairs in front of a blazing fire, continually refreshed by a succession of cups of tea made by the auctioneer's staff. Marooned by snow in a deserted mansion in the Black Mountains had seemed a minor adventure which he had looked forward to using as an anecdote but no one had been interested in that aspect of the affair. Instead, he and the other booksellers involved had been questioned as to whether their private auction afterwards had contravened the law. 'Frankly, I've had that story up to here. Really, Jake, do you think it possible that Bailey has me filed as someone open for shady deals on the strength of one rumour?'

'All right already.' Jake threw up his hands. 'I give in. I don't know why he picked you. But I'll tell you what. I don't think he was doing *you* a favour. Knowing Henry Bailey Esquire fairly well, that's out. How I see it, Mr A ...' Jake paused to show that he was still slightly irritated at not having been entrusted with Mr A's identity. 'Mr A wants an agent. Bailey's too busy but volunteers to find him one for him. And for no reason, just a mere whim, he suggests the only bookseller he knows who has a broken nose.'

'You win, Jake.'

The pastrami had arrived and looked very good. Jake picked up a dill pickle and reduced its size by half with one bite. He munched it thoughtfully and asked in a mock humble voice, 'And now, may I ask you one question. What is Mr A like? How did you react to him?'

'Very wealthy, subtle, shrewd. So intelligent he nearly manages to disguise the fact that he's rather obsessed with sex. I mean he's got the motto *Vivat lingam non resurgam* engraved on a silver tray, on his decanter and glasses. You would have to be a little odd, rather off-balance, to do things like that surely? But when he talks he smoothes it over with the gloss of keen intelligence.'

'Interesting. You know in an otherwise unspotted bookselling career, with nary a whisper of any 'ring' business, I've contacted a few high-powered collectors of erotica myself. Even sold one or two items to King Farouk. And with each one I had a curious feeling – of emptiness – they seemed to live poised over an abyss. Lives founded on nothing, in which they escaped the void only by giving themselves up to a kind of mania. There was a famous nineteenth century collector like that, you know. Frederick Hankey, in the 1860s, lived in rooms in the Rue Lafitte, near the Place de l'Opéra, which were cluttered with obscene objects. He was absolutely obsessed, poor devil . . .' Jake stopped to watch someone going past outside, his eyes slowly traversing the restaurant's window from right to left.

'Mighty odd. Did you see that big chap? I noticed him in King Street just before I caught up with you. Could it be you've got the law on your trail? That's what comes, I'm afraid, of being mixed up in the 'ring' and purveying erotica to Mr A.'

Howard went over to the window and looked out. Jake called out, 'In a dark blue or black coat, collar turned up. Brown fedora.' Howard stood staring at the lunch-time crowds making their way up towards Marylebone High Street, but could not see the man Jake had described.

9

Going down the escalator at Bond Street tube station, on his
way to Bina Gardens, Howard experienced a momentary sensation of panic. It was the first time he had been on the Underground since Meg had been killed and he had expected it to be
an occasion for unpleasant memories and thoughts, but a com-
pulsion he had to physically fight against, an overwhelming
desire to turn about and run up the ever-descending stairs, was
something he had never known before. He had been afraid often
in the war but this unreasoning fear was different, inducing an
absurd nervous fluttering in his chest. When he stumbled off the
escalator his legs felt numb and he moved mechanically along
white-tiled corridors which appeared endless. The sound of
footsteps and the rumble of trains echoed dully in his ears as if
taking place far away. Once in a boxing-match he had been
knocked flat on the canvas, could hear a disembodied voice
counting him out, had the will to get up but had not been able
to make his legs work. Now he experienced a similar difficulty in
breaking out from this nightmarish mood, like an attempt to
shake off the effects of an anaesthetic. He forced himself to
stand still, at first indifferent to what passers-by might think,
then pretending to study a poster advertising a Christmas Circus, while he brought himself under control.

His mind had always shied away from thinking of the details
of Meg's death, the actual fall, and her final terrifying vision of
the train relentlessly approaching, the horrible mutilation. Now
at last he considered all these things.

There are depths of human misery so profound that while
one descends they appear bottomless, but as Howard stared at
the meaningless details on the out-of-date poster, his eyes following the black print on yellow paper without making proper
sense of it, he plumbed his feelings of terror and guilt over
Meg's last moments. Then, to his surprise, in facing them the
horror ebbed away, leaving him strangely calm and dispas-
sionate. He became continually more certain that it must have
been an accident. There had not been one occasion in their

twenty years together when Meg had given any hint that she might take her own life. This had all been probed at the inquest and a verdict of misadventure had been returned. Only his guilty knowledge of his feelings for Catherine Gurney and a suspicion that Meg might be aware of how he felt had prevented him from believing that falling on the railway line was a terrible mischance. It was true that she had been in a strange mood that day but there could be many explanations for that. He could see now that a miasma of self-torment induced by guilt had held him captive for weeks.

As he began to walk along the corridor again the significance of the recurring dream about the Pembrokeshire holiday was suddenly revealed to him: it came into his mind as simply as if he had opened a lock. On that far off holiday he and Meg had talked endlessly on all kinds of subjects. Suicide had been one of them, and now quite clearly he could hear Meg stating flatly that where children were involved suicide was a cruel act that could never be justified. Regaining this memory was a curious irreversible process: once retrieved he could not understand why it had so long eluded him. Some perverse desire for punishment seemed the only solution.

Standing on the station platform Howard was able to look steadily about him. The dark opening of the tunnel, the rushing sound of the oncoming train which he had known in nightmares so real as to seem tangible experiences, lacked menace. When he got into the train he was set free to think of other things. Without a sense of guilt everything about him seemed slightly different, as if he had discarded distorting glasses.

Howard walked out of Earls Court Station feeling more optimistic and forward looking than he had for months. In this mood he believed that he had a good chance of finding Nancy Douce, and was determined to do everything he could regardless of how much time it would take.

I want to help: he repeated this phrase mentally and was buoyed up by its simple affirmation. He had no religious beliefs and thought that Dickie Carew's theory of the sand dollar, 'a stone-dead heart of things' alien to man's spiritual longings, might well be true. But, free of the guilt that had intermittently dogged him, life was once again its own justification.

84

Human relationships were what mattered in his life and gave it a meaning. Nina Douce had appeared to have confidence in his ability to solve the riddle about Nancy, and he was loath to disappoint her.

The Earls Court Road was full of people shopping, dwarfed to the appearance of mice by their numbers. Howard wondered what sort of impression this rather seedy part of London would have made on Nancy, fresh from the idyllic scenery of Grenada, then remembered that she would at least have seen it first in the autumn when there would have been leaves on the plane trees and possibly some sunshine. Today, under a uniformly grey sky, it appeared bleak indeed. The bitter wind had dropped but sleet was making the pavements greasy and it looked as if it might snow again at any moment.

As he turned into Bolton Gardens Howard went over in his mind what he knew about Nancy. Getting the picture clear might help him to think what she would do in certain circumstances. He had a photograph in his pocket, but he knew also that much of her attractiveness came from her colouring. 'Big dark brown eyes and blue-black hair: skin that looks as if it was perfectly tanned – a stunning combination' had been Meg's comment in her journal. Nancy was of slight build but full of energy, a rather restless person eager for new experiences. Suddenly he recalled the two little coloured girls, aged about ten and twelve, who had come to England on his flight. Inadequately dressed in summer frocks and cardigans, they had stood on the steps leading down from the plane looking round with great big eyes at all the lights of London Airport as if they had been transported to a wonderland. He had found it hard to visualize how it appeared to them. Probably to Nancy too, after a rather restricted island life, London had appeared exciting, full of the promise of new friends and opportunities.

He paused across the road from the house where Nancy had taken rooms. 'Brompton Lodge' in Bina Gardens was an unprepossessing five storied building of red brick with wrought iron trellises guarding narrow verandas on four floors and a Gothic-revival porch painted white. After he had rung the bell three times the door was opened by the landlord, Patterson, whom Howard recalled by his sausage-like fingers and pullover tucked into his trousers. Patterson had a face it would be impossible to remember and colourless hair to match. He also had an expression of deferential ennui – the look of someone who knows that nothing very interesting is going to happen.

'My name's Howard. I don't like bothering you but I'm wondering if you can tell me *anything* to help me trace Nancy Douce. Do you remember I called about some letters for her which you forwarded to me?'

Patterson nodded listlessly and took a slow motion step back. 'Do you want to come in? Draughty. This business is still going on then?'

'What business?'

Patterson snorted. 'All these questions. Some chap rang up from the West Indies about her at the weekend. Got quite excited when I said we had no address for her and couldn't help him. Told me he would be informing the police, so I explained they already knew . . .'

'The police know?' Howard felt confused by this turn of events; disappointed that he had not been relied upon to make the inquiries, and baffled by the police already having been called in.

Patterson turned away saying, 'Won't be a jiff', and went through a door. All his movements were marked by an economy of effort as if it was important for him to conserve energy. When he came back he held a note-pad by the tip of one corner, looking at it and nodding slightly. He read in an expressionless voice: 'Saturday evening. Mr Richard Carew phoned on behalf of Mrs Douce, to inquire regarding her daughter Nancy. Replied that she had left here and her address not known.'

Howard said: 'I'm puzzled. First of all I was told that you didn't have a phone. But more important, how did the police come on the scene before Mr Carew phoned?'

'It's all quite simple really. We have a phone but it's in my wife's room here and she's an invalid, confined to her chair. Osteo-arthritis in her legs. So we can't have the girls using it. They'd keep barging in . . .' He paused as if that was all the information he was going to supply.

'And the police?'

Patterson had a quizzical expression as though Howard had

asked a naïve question. 'The police? – well, frankly, what's that got to do with you? I mean you're not a relative are you? Didn't you say when you came before that you hadn't even met the girl?'

'That's true, but Mrs Douce, Nancy's mother, has asked me to make inquiries.' Howard handed over Mrs Douce's letter to Patterson, who made no attempt to undo the envelope but stood weighing it on his plump palm. After a few moments' reflection he said, 'I'll ask Mrs P. She knows more about this business than I do. Hold on.'

Howard looked round the hall which was decorated with some dusty Hogarth prints and an absurd Victorian oil-painting titled 'The Elopement', in which a large group of men were all striking dramatic attitudes. There was a pervasive smell of curry in the passage way which was cluttered up with a very large hallstand and a dining trolley, but the pitch pine floor and the solid elm staircase were clean and highly polished.

Patterson appeared, silently beckoning. His short, solid, graceless body hovered in the doorway as if he lacked energy to move either forward or back. His face was impassive but he managed to convey the impression that he was sighing inwardly. As Howard moved towards the door Patterson raised a fat finger of warning. 'Keep it short. She tires easily.'

It was an invalid's room, warm and airless, with bottles of medicine, tablets, and fruit squashes disposed on two small trolleys. Papers and magazines littered the floor by an unmade bed. In the corner on a silent television screen a vivacious woman was demonstrating how to cook something. The only wall decoration was a framed poker-work text: 'Him that cometh to Me I will in no wise cast out. *John*, vi, 37.' Mrs Patterson sat propped up by numerous cushions in a large armchair beside the bed. She wore a light blue wool dressing-gown and her legs were covered with a rug the same colour. A fresh smell of eau-de-cologne masked something less pleasant.

Mrs Patterson flashed a smile that did not reach her puffy eyes, and nervously touched her blonded hair. Her face had just been made up: beyond the normal outline of her lips she had painted on a Joan Crawford mouth. She indicated a chair close to her own. 'Do sit down, Mr Howard. You understand we should like to help Mrs Douce if we could. I'm just sorry that Nancy is giving her all this trouble and worry. I don't understand it . . .'

Howard sat down between Mrs Patterson and a pot of Turk's-head lilies that had a voluptuous, heavy perfume. 'And I'm very sorry to bother you like this, but we should like to know exactly when Nancy left. Whether she gave any indication where she might go. Anything like that.'

Mrs Patterson rummaged about in a large cardboard carton: 'I've got Nancy's rent-book here somewhere. We keep all the old ones because of our accounts and the income tax.' She opened a little paper-covered book in an exaggeratedly genteel way. Her nails were long and enamelled silver. She used her hands a lot, with delicate movements of arched fingers, as if to stress her feminine nature and oppose her wretched predicament. Howard was trying to imagine what it must be like to live confined to one room. In such a plight it would be difficult to take much interest in the movements of lively young lodgers.

Mrs Patterson frowned so that her dry powdered forehead became corrugated with lines. 'I should say the last time *I* saw Nancy was on the tenth of December when she paid the rent. But I know that Mrs Hodges, one of our cleaners, saw her on the 14th. Apparently that was Nancy's last day here as the bed wasn't slept in that night.'

'December 14th was the day Nancy last wrote to her mother.'

Mrs Patterson nodded judicially. 'She just upped and left. Didn't say a word to anybody about the why and wherefore. A week or so later a nice young man called in and gave me a note from Nancy saying she was moving and asking me to let him take her stuff away. He paid the rent, including a week in lieu of notice. Mrs Hodges helped him pack Nancy's bags and off he went. She didn't have much.'

'Isn't that unusual? Having someone else to collect her things.'

'Unusual!' Patterson snorted. He had been standing idly by as if not involved up to this point. He blew out air through compressed lips to express his bottled-up irritation. 'Well, what's usual with girls? You tell us. We never know what they're going to do next. Coming, going. Trying to smuggle boys into their rooms. Landing up in the family way. And this is just a business for us, you know? We're not their keepers.'

'No, let's be fair, I like to be fair,' Mrs Patterson interjected. 'There was nothing like that with Nancy. A nice quiet girl. Well behaved as far as I know.'

'The young man didn't say where Nancy was going? I mean whether it was elsewhere in London. He didn't mention Paris?'

'Nothing. Good-looking chap. Mid-twenties. Tall, fair-haired. Very polite, helpful. Kept on apologizing for any trouble that Nancy had given by moving out without giving notice.'

'Your husband mentioned something about the police having been called in.'

'Ah yes, that would be about ten days or a fortnight later. Anyway it was after you were here about the letters. A plain-clothes man. He said it was a routine check, something to do with her work permit. When we told him Nancy had gone he asked questions like you. We told him that our cleaner Mrs Hodges had said Nancy had given up her job some time before she left us, and that the only address she had mentioned in this country was your wife's at Henley. He made some notes about it. He was interested about you calling as we didn't know any of her other friends.'

Howard was struck by an odd thought. On the previous day there had been the 'big chap' whom Jake Wells had spotted in King Street and outside the Stage Door. Before his trip to Grenada, there was the man waiting outside Jill Lammas's flat. Hadn't the owl-eyed man in Pimlico said something about being on duty which Howard had dismissed as nonsense?

'What was the policeman like? Was he tall?'

Patterson said 'Yes, tall' in a very impatient way to stress that he was tired of dealing with stupid questions.

Howard got up and thanked Mrs Patterson. It struck him again how fortunate he was just to be able to get up and walk out of that enervating atmosphere. As he went into the hall he said to Patterson: 'One more question and I'll go. It's strange but I feel I may have bumped into that policeman. Did he have an Australian accent?'

'No. Not Australian. We've got an Australian girl here so I would have remembered that I'm sure. Oh, there's Mrs

Hodges, our cleaner, we mentioned. She *might* be able to help. Mrs Hodges, this is Mr Howard. He's trying to trace that West Indian girl, Nancy Douce, you remember?'

Patterson urged Howard along the dark passage-way leading to the back of the house where Mrs Hodges stood at the top of the basement stairs, then turned on his heel with an abbreviated wave of his hand.

Mrs Hodges watched this manoeuvre with obvious amusement and giggled when Patterson had gone. 'Ted's a one ain't he. Never three words where two will do. Come on downstairs. I've got a kettle on.'

Howard followed her down steep unlit stairs into a large room which contained a scrubbed deal table, an old-fashioned sink, and a gas-stove. The curry smell gradually merged into a vaguely institutional one of floor polish and soap. Mrs Hodges hurried over to the boiling kettle and poured the water into a teapot. 'There! We'll have a cuppa.' She turned about to face Howard with a rueful expression. There was something about the way she looked at him that made Howard feel he might find out more from her about Nancy than he had done with the Pattersons. She was approximately his own age, in her early forties, and plump but still attractive with a wonderful complexion and a mass of red curling hair. Her eyes were lively and she looked as if she enjoyed everything she did. 'I don't know where Nancy is. She did a moonlight you know? They ...' – she gave an expressive shrug and shake of her head upwards – 'wouldn't know what she was up to of course. Mrs P. she just does the clerical and hardly sees the girls at all. And Ted's kept pretty busy to-ing and fro-ing for her. They haven't got time to chat or so they say. But I love a natter so naturally I was hurt Nancy didn't say nothing. She used to tell me a lot about her home. It sounds smashing. All that sunshine, everybody happy and gay, cheap rum and lovely fruit. She was always going on about people in the streets here not smiling, looking so miserable. And the fruit not tasting like it did in the West Indies. You see, the grapefruits and the bananas we have, they nearly all come from over there. Just seeing that Geest label on the bananas made her homesick she said. Of course it made a difference her being so friendly with your wife. She was always mentioning her – Mrs Howard says this, Mrs Howard says that.'

Howard somehow could not bring himself to tell her that Meg was dead. His reluctance to broach the subject could lead him into an even more embarrassing position later but he let the opportunity pass, asking instead: 'What did you think of the young man who called for her things?'

Mrs Hodges' eyes sparkled; she smiled and moved her head from side to side to express a favourable reaction. 'Ooh, swinging. Good-looking Chelsea type – you know – tall with long fair hair. Suede boots and trousers as tight as that ballet dancer Nureyev wears. Very polite. Bags of charm ...' Her face became serious. 'Course, Nancy knows some funny ones too. "A queer crew" one of the other girls here called them. I mean that's what may have led to this trouble, don't you think? She's been spoilt a bit I suppose. Getting so much attention.'

'Who was it said that Nancy knew a queer crew? Do you think she might be able to tell me anything about her friends?'

'No, that was Susan Hardy, kept herself to herself. Anyway, she's gone back to Manchester now. She only saw Nancy coming back here late one night and the people in two flash cars who brought her.' Mrs Hodges busied herself in pouring out two cups of very strong, well-brewed tea. 'Sugar?' she asked, then flashed her free hand up to her mouth in a childish gesture of being caught out, with one finger pressed against her lower lip. 'Ooh, there was something. I've still got Nancy's note-pad. It was among a pile of old magazines we threw out and there's lots of unused pages so I kept it for shopping lists.' She stepped across the room to a cupboard which contained a shelf above a space for brooms and a vacuum cleaner. 'There are one or two names on the cover, but yours is the only address. Mainly just scribbling.' She shook her head vigorously, bringing down a few more curls. 'Funny girl. The things she writes down.'

Howard looked at the inside of the pad's paper flap. Below his Henley address there was a skilful drawing of a yacht together with random jottings. ' "Moon river" – "Two drifters, off to see the world/There's such a lot of world to see". Dio Boia – the Hangman God. Quasars – a thousand million miles away. "As rich as Midas" – Sir Giorgius Midas (Victorian multi-millionaire). Norfolk Howard – slang for bedbug (O.E.D.): from Joshua Bug, Norfolk landowner who changed his name to Norfolk Howard.'

Apart from the note about his own name most of the phrases had little more significance for him than they did for Mrs Hodges, but at the bottom there were two names he knew. 'Larry Paton – party at Park Place. Larry – Quincy's warning!'

Larry Paton had only been a shadowy figure in Meg's journal about Grenada, mentioned briefly without any description as being on board Carew's yacht. But his name, together with other enigmatic phrases on the note-pad, could be the key to Nancy's disappearance. It was quite possible that, despite Quincy's warning about Paton, he and Nancy were the 'two drifters, off to see the world'. The more Howard thought about this the more likely it became – if Nancy had gone off with a man of whom she knew her mother would not approve, it could easily have led to this worrying period of silence. At least this gave him something to work on: he could try to find an address in England for Paton or, failing that, write to Mrs Douce suggesting that Paton should be contacted.

Howard said, 'Do you mind if I keep this page? It might be helpful.' When Mrs Hodges nodded he pocketed it, again feeling quite optimistic about the chances of finding Nancy in no worse circumstances than those in which Jill Lammas somehow survived. It was rather odd that he should be trying to find one young girl while for all he knew Jill Lammas's father might be doing the same, tracking her down one night to a flat over a bookshop in New Cavendish Street.

Mrs Hodges gulped some tea down and grimaced knowingly, mirroring some of his wry thoughts with her final comment: 'Not to worry. Nancy will be all right! Lots of young girls get up to some funny capers, but they come out the other side okay.'

10

Tuesday, February 18th, 1969. It was a mild day with a dramatic sky in which great clouds moved continually towards the north-east with occasional shafts of pale sunlight. Howard had arrived in Swains Lane, Highgate, nearly twenty minutes too early for his appointment to meet Miss Edith Voysey so he walked past the cemetery gates and up the hill. He would have been hard put to it the day before in the Earls Court area to occupy himself agreeably in strolling, but this part of Highgate was pleasant enough with a long weathered brick wall on his left hand that might have surrounded a large country estate. All around him he noticed birds on their urgent winter tasks, but a thin thrush was perched in a bare ash tree singing away as if to corroborate the promise of spring in the mild sunshine.

It was only ten days since Howard had heard from Catherine Gurney but he knew that this meant their love affair was over. He could see the irony of his dithering about how to suggest ending their secret relationship when she must already have decided to do so. For her it had involved only the negative act of not communicating with him, as the initiative regarding writing and telephoning had always been in her hands alone.

Howard stared at the stormy sky, watching how a streak of primrose changed to grey then indigo, remembering an evening in the previous November which he and Catherine had spent in walking on Hampstead Heath while Catherine told him about the different positions of the stars in the winter and summer skies. There would be no more meetings like that – no more walks with their arms round each other like young lovers – no more poignant good-byes – no more foolish excitement in opening a letter or planning a rendezvous.

This knowledge made him sad and empty but he felt he was in a better position to accept it than before his trip to Grenada. Getting away then had enabled him to stand off and observe himself in a more detached way. Before, he had thought that Meg and he had simply outgrown each other, but now he could see that the fault definitely lay in his own personality. Meg had grown up, becoming a mature person willing to accept their life as it had evolved over a period of twenty years; but he had found the repetition and ordinariness unbearable and longed for the excitement of romantic love. A dream he had about Catherine was symptomatic. In the dream he had driven for miles along empty snow-covered roads to reach her. When he abandoned the car he had to struggle through deep snow in a landscape made spectral by moonlight until he saw the cottage where he knew she was waiting for him. The small unlit house stood on a hill surrounded by even deeper drifts which he had to fight his way through, and by the time he entered the door his heart was beating so loudly it sounded like a clock.

His relationship with Catherine had always been on that idealized, slightly unreal basis. They had never discussed the future beyond their next meeting, as that was all they could plan. They really knew very little about each other and that, of course, had been part of the fascination. And all the thwarting circumstances added to it. What had Curtis Mahon said about 'wanting nothing unless we felt cheated out of it'. Their brief meetings had really been only a series of gestures against the routine of their daily lives.

Howard laughed to himself on thinking how ruthlessly Jill would deal with all this. The dream would be dismissed as simple sexual frustration and she would say that in embarking on such a hopeless affair he was simply acting out a Peter Pan syndrome, or something like that. Jill was sure to know an up-to-date psychological label for that kind of thing. She had a sure eye for other people's foibles even though she could not cure her own 'hang-ups', which made her often unable to sleep till the early hours and prevented her from getting up before mid-day.

Howard contemplated the overwhelming task involved if someone were to fall in love with Jill and wanted to bring a reasonable amount of order into her life. She admitted it was 'sheer chaos, instant improvisation' at the moment. She had cleverly evaded his questions about what jobs she had tried, mentioning only occasionally helping a friend who had an antique shop in the Camden Passage off Upper Street in Islington. If this were true then it was one of a mere handful of facts, such as her being left-handed and the address in Pimlico, that he knew about her. All the other information she had given him was of a negative nature. She admitted to not having paid any income tax or stamped her insurance card for over a year, and to some vague 'trouble with the authorities'. She said she was not in communication with her family or anyone she had known before coming to London. She had not registered with a doctor.

Suddenly it struck Howard that if Jill Lammas were to disappear it would be as difficult a task to trace her as it was with Nancy Douce. He felt certain his own relationship with her was bound to be short-lived. She had said she would come to New Cavendish Street later that night so he had given her a key, but he would not be surprised if he never saw her again. 'Poor Cinderella will be struggling up the old corkscrew stairs at midnight.' Perhaps. The gulf between their generations was too wide to be bridged satisfactorily. Every carefree young sprig, each youth he saw in casual clothes with a happy-go-lucky air seemed to be a more suitable partner than he was for Jill Lammas.

Howard recalled her expression of suppressed boredom as she searched through his collection of records. 'What no Frugs!' she had exclaimed. 'Never mind, darling, we'll have to settle for Old King Cole.' In fact the only things he had in common with Jill were a strong sexual drive and a sense of the absurd.

They came together in the physical act of love-making like two drowning people, with something of desperation in their desire to lose themselves in each other. In the previous evening they had fallen off the couch in the midst of sexual congress, continuing on the floor in a frenzy of desire. She attained her climax with a deep shudder and frantic movements of her hands on his back. Then an indefinable, sweet expression came into her eyes while her features took on a delicate nature in the 'little death'. 'Dear absolute gain' she breathed into his ear.

Minutes later, as they still lay enjoined, the incongruity of their position, spreadeagled on a carpet, the actuality of their sweating bodies and pounding hearts as distinct from the glimpse of Nirvana, struck them both. 'You are hereby awarded a badge for depravity ...' she said, pausing for effect. 'Second class.' She giggled and then began to shake with silent laughter. As she tried helplessly to stop laughing, rippling movements passed from her body to his own until they were both convulsed with laughter which became quite painful.

It was odd not knowing whether Jill would be with him in bed again that night, lying as close as two spoons in a drawer, whispering foolish nothings, or gone from his life.

Howard turned round at the top of the lane and looked back towards the cemetery gate. There was no one in sight but it was only five minutes to four. Far away in the north-west direction he could see patches of sunlight moving across a hill, changing its colour from dark grey to sage green; near at hand he noticed the spiral shadows cast on the wall by tendrils of ivy.

As he started to walk down the hill a crow shot up on the other side of the wall, looking like a black angel in its hasty ascent. Howard had spent the morning closeted in his book-shop making a list of seventeenth-century theological pamphlets and would probably return to it in the evening – now he sniffed the fresh air appreciatively, grateful for an excuse to escape the task for a few hours. The journey to Highgate had been worth-while even if Miss Voysey did not make an appearance. It had been futile to speculate about her reason for wanting to meet him so he had deliberately shut it out of his mind, but it seemed unlikely to be a matter of such importance; probably Miss Voysey had known Meg years ago and then had lost touch with her till she had read of her death.

When Howard reached the gate again there was no elderly lady in a blue coat waiting for him. A small boy, dressed in a school cap and over-long mackintosh, was walking round and round in a circle kicking a stone. Howard looked pointlessly at his watch and then read a notice about the cemetery being closed at five p.m. when a bell would be rung. The boy was watching him and said: 'Are you Mr Howard? Miss Voysey asked me to explain she couldn't come, but I can show you the hotel.' Apparently a volte-face had taken place and Calvert's Hotel was no longer forbidden ground. Howard thanked the boy and followed him.

Howard could remember reading somewhere that a number of celebrated people were buried in Highgate Cemetery and had expected it to be rather a show place, but it appeared to be as run-down as most country grave-yards with long coarse grass growing on the graves and briars springing up between them. On the right of the mossy path he noticed a gloomy mausoleum with a coat of arms and the engraved words 'Dalziel of Wooler'. A row of poplar trees was threshing about in the strong south-west wind as the sky darkened rapidly.

The boy forgot his stone for a moment to turn and stare at Howard with unconcealed curiosity. When this probing was finished he said, 'D'you know this place?' Howard shook his head. The boy's face showed a flickering expression of pleasure or superiority. 'See that chap there. The one with the big head. That's Karl Marx. He's famous. Lots of people come here and stand round looking at that head.'

It was indeed a massive head, cast in black metal, set on grey marble blocks. It looked rather out of place among all the angels, crosses, and conventional stones, as did the message in large gilt Roman letters: WORKERS OF THE WORLD UNITE . . . There was no one standing round looking at it but there were some fresh wreaths and a framed message in red Cyrillic lettering. Howard tried to see the place through the boy's eyes. What impressions would he be taking in now, and what did he make of this odd errand? Howard regretted that he was out of practice in talking to children (when he had em-barked on telling one of the little Gurney girls about Cinderella he found he had forgotten most of the story and had to pad it out with his own inventions), though he had once seemed to have the knack of communicating with them. The boy had lost his stone and took a vicious running kick at a bedraggled chrysanthemum. When he had ground this satisfactorily into the path he called out over his shoulder: ' 'Tisn't far now. We just go down that lane. Brings you round the back. *You* mustn't go in the front.' He appeared to have been well drilled by Miss Voysey.

As they walked along the muddy lane Howard asked the boy if he lived in Calvert's Hotel and received an incredulous stare. 'Me?' said the boy. 'Not likely. Coo, I wouldn't live there. Not for . . .' His imagination seemed to be over-taxed by estimating the necessary incentive. 'It smells of moth-balls.' He wheeled about. 'That's it. Miss Voysey's waiting. I've got to go now.' Howard handed the boy a shilling and he ran off.

A small green gate opened into a run-down garden where the lawn was largely mud and a diamond-shaped flower-bed containing only the straw-like remains of lobelia plants and frost-blackened stalks of dahlias. There was a single row of strong-smelling cabbages and a pile of damp bean haulms which had resisted a bonfire. A long line of sheets billowed about, looking as if they might fly off with the south-west wind at any moment.

The house was a tall gingerbread affair with fanciful turrets on the top floor and two circular windows like giant monocles, an Edwardian art nouveau dream which had become a bad joke. The original building had been encumbered with an annexe squashed on to its side and a crazy-looking fire escape. There seemed to be more pipes than the plumbing could justify. A large wooden veranda was attached to the second floor, with steps leading down into the garden. Someone was waving from the door of a small conservatory.

When Howard was near to the glass door a woman darted out with an uncertain movement and seized his hand momentarily. She was wearing a black cardigan and a blue woollen dress long enough to be classified by Jill Lammas as a 'maxi'. She had coarse black hair that had turned pure white at the temples. She shot him a nervous, appraising look as she fingered a garnett brooch at her throat. Her eyes were bright and surprisingly young-looking. 'Poor Mr Howard. I do apologize. All this rigmarole! But you'll understand later. I thought from your voice you were sympathetic, that's why I decided after all that it would be all right for you to come here. It's been such a business. For the first time in weeks, *today* Mother suddenly decides to come downstairs for tea. So I couldn't get away. Then I was frightened she might pop out and ask some awkward questions. You see, I can't lie to her even if I don't always tell her everything. So I asked Wilson to manage things so that Mother waits a little while for her tea to give me a chance to smuggle you in. It's been a matter of split-timing. Rather like a French farce . . .' She smiled tentatively. She was in her sixties but there was just a glimpse of the young girl whom Time had been busy disguising with cross-hatching of lines and hollows in her cheeks which exaggerated the strength of the central part of her chin, giving it a Punch-like effect.

Miss Voysey swung about awkwardly, looking at him nervously again, and Howard noticed that she was leaning on a silver-headed stick with a thick rubber ferrule at the base. 'If you'll follow me, Mr Howard. I've arranged that we shall have some tea in the summer lounge overlooking the garden. It will be empty and we can talk there undisturbed.'

They went through the conservatory with its faint smell of geraniums and then along a feebly lit long passage, the walls of which were practically filled with native shields, spears, old photographs, and two mangy-looking tiger-skins. At the end of the dim passage she paused. 'This sounds absurd, but will you wait a moment while I see if everything is as it should be. I'm sorry to have to treat you like a conspirator. I'll explain it all very soon.' She made a brief despairing gesture.

Howard examined the patchwork of trophies. About some of the solemn studies of hunters standing triumphantly by fallen beasts there was the ludicrous aspect of knowing that they too were now dust, but others he found touching. He was intrigued by an excellent group photograph inscribed in copperplate: 'Mr Pat Ramvaddy's Globe Trotters. Golf Club, Rangoon. 1890.' This showed a long row of men and women in white tropical clothes recorded in a moment of genuine gaiety with smiles on nearly every face. Howard studied the now deceased Globe Trotters one after another. They looked very lively, as if it might have been difficult for the photographer to restrain them long enough to pop under his black hood. An old type-written note, in faded purple letters, was stuck to the frame: 'The Globe Trotters were Service entertainers, very popular in the 1890s.'

Close to Howard's hand there was a barrel constructed from parchment stretched over a brass frame holding a large number of canes and sticks, dusty and obviously undisturbed for months. There was the faint smell of moth-balls which the boy had mentioned, the noise of someone moving very slowly overhead, and these together with the feeble light conjured up the sensation of tedious hours passed in Calvert's Hotel waiting for the gong to be rung announcing another meal.

Miss Voysey appeared again, nodding rapidly to indicate that everything was in order. As they slowly mounted some shallow stairs, she asked Howard, 'Do you know this kind of place?'

Howard answered, 'Yes I do. My work involves a lot of travelling, in fact I quarter the country, going to auctions of old books. So I'm often in hotels.' It was a discreet answer which avoided any comment on 'this kind of place' but he had often stayed at nearly identical hotels in Bath, Leamington and Cheltenham, where someone was always greeted at breakfast by 'Morning, Major!', where there were silent, long-standing vendettas between residents and chairs became regarded as private property. He knew the smell of the roast beef and cabbage lunches, the peppery taste of the Mulligatawny soup, the insipidity of the Brown Windsor, the trolley in the dining-room with bottles of Worcester Sauce, Yorkshire Relish, and jars of special chutneys bearing proprietary names one never saw in shops.

'We don't live here permanently,' Miss Voysey hastened to explain. 'We have a small cottage in Suffolk. We came here in December intending to stay just till the New Year then – well, Mother became ill and I couldn't cope with her in Snape by myself . . .'

She glanced at a sepia photograph of Mr Algy Lawley and the Ganges Cup Hunt in 1880. 'We've been coming here so long we don't notice things that must seem odd to people used to modern places. My father was in the Army in India. When we came on leave to the U K he always called this his winter base. Overstrand in Norfolk was the summer one. The Overstrand hotel we used to stay at has disappeared – it simply fell into the sea. The cliff eroded . . .' She appeared vague and puzzled for a moment, as if she could not cope with a world in which nothing was permanent. She looked up and down to make sure there was no one else on the stairs. 'Of course it's not so comfortable here as it used to be. They can't get staff.'

They entered the summer lounge, a large room with a high ceiling inadequately lit by two lamps on long flexes. Heating was provided by a small gas-fire. All the furniture was made of cane or bamboo, and two cane chairs had been pushed close to the fire. There was a tray of tea things. The uncurtained dark french windows opening on to the wooden veranda were being rattled constantly by the wind. Miss Voysey looked round and shivered. 'Oh dear. Thank goodness there's tea. One does get to depend on it terribly.'

Howard passed the plate of bread and butter to Miss Voysey and opened a miniature jar of jam for her, then sat back. He had not attempted to prompt her reason for wishing to see him but did not feel inclined to delay it further with general conversation. Miss Voysey offered him a slice of yellow cake and sipped her tea. The silence between them lengthened and became oppressive. Howard began to wonder if he should broach the matter after all when she leant across the small table and touched his hand with the tips of her cold fingers. She looked frightened and oddly guilty. 'Courage!' she said. 'This may come as a shock I'm afraid.' She looked into the gas-fire's glow as if she were thinking hard. 'When – when your wife was killed, Mr Howard. That terrible day. We were there, Mother and I. Standing right next to her on the platform, waiting for that train.'

Howard felt slightly sick at this jolting reminder of the way in which Meg had died but other feelings contended in his mind, extreme irritation being the one uppermost. No eye witnesses of the accident had come forward. People on the platform who had been questioned by the police claimed not to have seen Meg's actual fall. A detective sergeant who had talked to him about it had not been surprised at this, explaining that 'the public was always reluctant' to be involved in the aftermath of such matters. 'If they can help there and then, first aid and suchlike. Yes, that kind of thing, all right. But courts, police, witnesses, questions? – they just don't want to know. And then again Christmas, you see. It'll sound fantastic to you but the fact of it being Christmas would have made them even more reluctant to come forward.'

Howard wet his lips. 'If you were there then why didn't you tell the police?' His anger prompted other questions but he held them back.

'I knew you would be angry. I understand. I read that there

were no witnesses – in the papers. Please believe that I do know how you must feel. But what could I have done? It was my mother who saw what happened, not me. I was looking the other way, towards the train. Mother fainted so I did not know exactly what she had seen. Then you can imagine the commotion, and Mother was sprawled on the platform as people crowded round. Someone helped me to get her on the escalator. We came back here by taxi and I sent for a doctor. It was a terrible shock for her. The fool of a doctor said "Old ladies are notoriously tough." What an absurd thing to say!' Miss Voysey shook her head sadly. 'My mother is far from being tough. Quite the reverse; she's very sensitive, highly strung. And, how can I explain? There's that line in the song Paul Robeson sang: "Tired of living and scared of dying". That's my mother, Mr Howard. Afterwards she was physically ill – I can't go into details. But in the circumstances are you still surprised I did not go to the police? Surely you can see my dilemma?'

With the explanation Howard's anger had disappeared. 'Yes – I can see that. But it's been two months. Why tell me now?'

Miss Voysey sighed again. 'That's even more difficult. But please – as you hear me – don't think I haven't said anything before because I was indifferent. It wasn't a matter of not caring. In fact there hasn't been a single day when I've forgotten it. You see, my mother actually saw that a man caused your wife to fall. He came rushing blindly out of the passageway just as the train came in – lurched to one side and must have caught her off-balance. You can't imagine how I've wanted to say something about this. Just in case you had a suspicion of anything else. I've felt terrible about it . . .'

There had been dozens of occasions in the past weeks when Howard would have given anything to have the suspicion of suicide (with all the guilt it entailed for him) removed from his mind, but now that it had happened the relief was clouded with anger. As he envisaged the scene on the platform cold fury stirred in him and he wanted to strike down the clumsy oaf who had sent Meg sprawling. The useless and irrational feeling was so strong that he could not remain seated. He walked over to the window and looked out, momentarily resting his forehead against the cold glass. Somewhere in the darkness a dog was barking monotonously and the wailing sound echoed in his own sensation of profound loneliness. Out there in the winter night was the chasm, the emptiness that Jake Wells had talked about. His feeling of anger changed to one of formless fear, and for a minute or two he was lost in his thoughts until he remembered Miss Voysey and turned round to see her looking apprehensively at him. He was moved by her vulnerability and all the tension she had incurred just by happening to be at the scene of the accident.

He walked over to her, managing to smile. 'It's all right now. Don't worry about it any more. I'm glad you told me. Glad and *very* grateful. Please believe that.'

11

> For all we know
> This may only be a dream
> We come and go
> Like ripples on a stream
> For all we know
> We may never meet again . . .

Howard reached across and lifted the record-player arm with an abrupt snatching movement that scratched the disc. It was one of his favourite Nat King Cole records but he could not bear its poignancy in his present mood. He put on the Boulez recording of *La Mer* and drained the remains of the Mount Gay rum into his tumbler, topping it up with ginger ale. After seeing Miss Voysey he had called in on his mother, but had been hard put to it to make conversation about his West Indies trip. The memory of Grenada was already fading and it seemed inconsequential. Hardly anything mattered in a world ruled by mere chance where someone could fall to an unimaginably painful death because someone else was simply in a hurry to catch a train.

Howard picked up *Our Mutual Friend*, read one sentence about the Veneerings, and put it down. He was too restless and dissatisfied to settle to reading or the work he had planned to do. It was only 8.30 and there were at least three hours to kill before he could expect to see Jill.

On his desk Nancy Douce's books *The Tarot* and *The Magus*, which he had said he would take with him to Grenada and had then forgotten, lay like a dumb reproach. He re-read the cable which had come that afternoon in reply to his own to Carew: PLEASE TAKE UP NANCY'S DISAPPEAR-ANCE WITH POLICE AGAIN AND URGE SOME AC-TION PATON'S ADDRESS NOT KNOWN HERE MOST UNLIKELY HE CAN HELP REGARDS RICHARD CAREW.

Howard had searched all the telephone directories at the Leicester Square Post Office without finding a Larry Paton listed. He had decided he would go to Marylebone Lane Police Station early in the morning before he went to a house auction in Knightsbridge. In the afternoon he intended to go back to his house near Henley to fetch some clothes which Jacqueline had asked him to send to Paris. Once this dreary evening was over there was quite a lot to do to keep himself busy. It was simply a matter of getting through three or four hours in which every minute dragged. Making a snack for himself was as unattractive as having a meal out, but he decided to look in the refrigerator to see if Jill had bought anything.

As he walked into the kitchen the phone rang. It was Jill sounding as if she had drunk too much and was surrounded by others feeling equally hilarious. Her words were punctuated by giggling and there was a background of pop music. 'Dear Nick,' she began, collapsing into laughter as someone feebly added 'Dear Knickers'. 'Your presence is hereby requested. Here and herewith. No, make that forthwith.' A male voice commented 'All teeth and tits', and there was a series of half-smothered sniggers. Howard knew it was going to be difficult to refuse without sounding a spoil-sport. It was nice of her to want him to go. 'Jill – do you mind if I don't? I'm not really in the mood for a party ...'

'It's not a party. Just a few friends and they all want to meet you. Don't you, friends?' This appeal to her audience led to much scuffling and someone laughing helplessly as though being relentlessly tickled. Than another female voice came on, rich and imperious (there was just the hint of condescension, the heiress talking to the ski instructor): 'Now do listen! This is Domino. Jill's told me about you and I'm intrigued so you've got to come and that's that. Don't hang about.'

Jill said: 'Please come, Nick. I want you to. It's only round the corner from your place. Turn left into Harley Street at the lights and walk up to the top. It's the big white house facing the park. In need of a lick of paint and there's builder's scaffolding all over the place. You can't miss it.' The other girl added: 'We're all wearing masks and they just kill all inhibitions. The pass-word is domino.' Then the receiver was slammed down with a bang which echoed in his ear.

Within a few minutes Howard was walking along Harley Street. He felt that he was going to be out of place in a crowd of gay young people but anything was better than an evening of his own company. That, together with Jill sounding keen, had been enough to persuade him. She had called him Nick for the first time, and he preferred it to her ubiquitous and he suspected meaningless 'Darling'. If he wanted to continue seeing her he would undoubtedly have to make more and more effort as time went by to keep her interested, and probably would end up like Emil Jannings in *The Blue Angel* capering about at Marlene Dietrich's every whim.

Half-way along to the park Howard suddenly wanted to pee. The wind had swung round, again bringing an arctic chill to the London streets: the cold, nerves, and the rum he had drunk were conspiring against him. It seemed ludicrous to return to his flat for such a trifling reason, and equally absurd to arrive in a state of anxiousness about the location of a lavatory. The sight of the builder's scaffolding which signposted the house made him decide to go on.

When he had rung the bell once a finger appeared from the letter-box, pointing up at his face. An indistinct voice, constrained by laughter, said: 'First of all, before you say or do anything else – for Christ's sake! Take off that horrific mask.'

Even if he had been in a mood for jokes this one would not have convulsed Howard. It seemed best, however, to go along with it, so he shifted from one foot to another and pretended to have trouble wrenching something from his face.

The muffled voice sounded mollified. 'That's better, old man. Now what's the pass-word?'

'Domino.'

'It was but we changed it.' The door remained shut. 'My name's Belchamp. What's yours, old man?'

Howard bent down to look through the letter-box but could see only a painted papier-mâché nose. 'Squireens, old man. And I do need to come in. It's really quite urgent.'

The voice from the letter-box said 'This isn't a public convenience, old man,' but the frank appeal did the trick. The door opened, revealing a very thin, tall youth in black trousers and a black moiré shirt, wearing a devil's mask. He took this off to stare at Howard. An edge of white showed below his tawny pupils and he was obviously having difficulty in getting his eyes to focus. He held them closed for a few seconds but this did not seem to help. He talked quite sensibly. 'There's a place downstairs. Rather a fun one. And when you come up I'll show you something else slightly bizarre. All right?'

It was a distinctly grand hall with a superb stair-rail, fine enough to have been designed by Jean Lamour, but it was furnished like a set in a 1930s film. Light was thrown up to the ceiling from a large chrome standard-lamp. There was an outsize ebony chair and a circular glass table half covered with coats. Howard would not have been surprised to see Carol Lombard making an entrance, pausing with a hand on a marble pedestal that supported a Bouché figurine. On the wall going up the stairs there was a large drawing by Erté. Paint-splattered steps, floor coverings, and pots of brushes had been pushed into one corner. A subdued but continuous sound of music came from the floor above.

Howard stumbled on the stairs, going down too quickly, and laughed to himself. Did anyone else of his age ever get into such a predicament where finding somewhere to pee was of supreme importance? At the bottom of the stairs he found his quest ended, and he was faced by what looked like a miniature theatre cloak-room with two lavatories, two wash-basins, and a long rail of coat-hangers.

There was a musty smell about the house as if it had been closed up for years and only recently exposed to the decorators' re-furbishing. The washer had gone on the tap and it dripped ceaselessly. After he had washed his hands he noticed that there was a crack in the other green marble basin. Looking underneath it he found the pipes were wrapped in the grey of a spider's web: more swags of cobweb hung over the large spotted mirror.

Howard went back up the stairs slowly, noticing a fine Limoges *champlévé* enamel, a cover for a medieval book of Gospels showing Christ seated in majesty with the Evangelists in the four spandrels. It was a museum piece but it too was gathering a covering of dust.

When he returned to the hall the youth was waiting for him, still possessed by a mood of febrile gaiety and having trouble with his unfocused eyes. 'Okay now?' he asked with feeling. 'I know what it's like – it can be absolute aggers and torters. This way!' He darted off into a darkened room. 'How's this for show-biz baroque?'

The youth switched on a chrome lamp standing on top of a rose-wood pianola. Much of the furniture in the room was shrouded by dust-sheets but the pieces that stood revealed were of the same period as those in the hall. Along one wall there was an enormous radiogram of a type that Howard could remember seeing advertised at a fabulous price in pre-war American magazines. A geometrically designed black side-board was surmounted by a chrome fixture showing the long rays of a setting sun. There was another drawing by Erté of a woman in a hopelessly impractical evening dress and coat of black and white fur, the sleeves of which cascaded to the floor.

The youth looked round indulgently at the radio: 'You can only get old programmes on that, but listen to this.' He manipulated his hands and then switched on the pianola, playing it with gusto, spanning the moving keys with thin fingers and pedalling away strongly. 'Oh fit as a fiddle/And ready for love . . .' he sang in a quavering voice.

'Charming,' Howard said. 'But I think I ought to go upstairs. Someone's waiting for me.'

The youth frowned in concentration, straining to read the rapidly disappearing words. 'Wait a sec and I'll be with you. Just this bit. Now.' He turned round to ogle Howard for a moment and then sang in a simpering tone: 'Keep young and beautiful/It's your duty to be beautiful ... With some powder and a puff/Keep young and beautiful/If you want to be loved...'

Howard turned and walked away but the youth caught up with him at the bottom of the imposing stairs, proffering a tray on which there was an assortment of papier-mâché masks. 'They're rather good ones. They come from that J. H. Spaans shop near the Skin Hospital in Lisle Street.'

Howard's hand hovered in reluctance: finally he picked out an extremely large nose. The youth commented, 'That's interesting. Psychologically I mean. Your choice of that nose.'

'How do you mean?' Howard fitted the nose on and then felt its extended length. It would be difficult to look at anything else.

'Shows a latent aggressive trait. Cyrano de Bergerac said "Thank God, here comes another enemy." And I must say you look disgustingly fit and tough. The odd man out here.'

Howard grinned. 'You know what they say. Train hard – fight easy.'

'Who invited you here, old man?'

'Jill Lammas.'

'Ah August the 1st, the Pimlico Swinger. That explains a lot.'

Howard wanted to question the youth about this enigmatic statement but they were close to the source of music and laughter. The painting of this floor appeared to be completed and the passage-way they went along was pale blue, decorated with Greek plaster medallions. The youth was already jigging up and down to the music's strong beat. 'That was the Marmalade,' he explained. 'And that – ah, that's *Fox on the Run* by Manfred Mann.'

The large room they entered was on two levels. A long table covered with glasses and plates of canapés was on the upper part by the door. Howard waited by it, looking round anxiously for Jill, but the young man plunged down the stairs and into the melée of dancers. Howard took a glass of champagne and a smoked salmon sandwich. The dancers were mainly young girls prancing around in a self-absorbed ritualistic fashion. Most of them were wearing dominos rather than full masks, but one was concealed by a horrific white one with vivid red gashes. The lower floor was lit by coloured lights while a bank of spotlights reflected by rotating mirrors contrived the so-called 'Psyche-delic' effect.

'How about that?' A man with an unpleasant empurpled visage and gold-crusted lizard-like eyes touched Howard's arm and then gestured sweepingly at the dancing throng. 'A las-civious grace in which all evil shows well. I must say I rather fancy that little dolly.' He pointed to a girl with very long blonde hair whose contortions were particularly energetic and displayed flowered briefs at the tops of white stockings. 'You see,' the man said in a rather husky voice, 'once upon a time there was this chap who had the seven year itch – no, the four-teen year itch – that's twice as bad . . .' He brooded in silence on the blonde girl and Howard moved farther along the table while searching the room for Jill.

A girl with suspiciously black hair and a silver domino that did not disguise her nervousness said to Howard: 'What on earth would all this cost?' pointing at about four dozen un-opened bottles of Champagne de Saint Marceaux standing on ice in a large bin. A coloured man in evening dress was occupied continuously in filling glasses while a coloured woman replenished the plates of little open sandwiches. 'The mind simply boggles. Oh well, they're not going to send me the bill.'

Another girl, with long tawny hair and greeny-yellow eyes, dressed in a lamé blouse and black trousers, came close to Howard, her lips shaping a silent word. The lizard man had approached to take a pâté sandwich, and toasted them 'Bottoms up!' The girl with cat's eyes said 'Promises! promises!' with-out enthusiasm, then she gripped Howard's right arm, squeez-ing his biceps. 'I'm Domino, Jill's friend.'

'That's good!' Howard exclaimed with relief. 'Is Jill here too?'

'Jill Lammas the Pimlico Swinger?' the lizard man inquired. 'She's here all right, smelling like scented lavatory cleaner. What's that stuff? Po pourried?'

Howard turned to the lizard man: 'Flutter off.'

The lizard man swallowed some more champagne. 'Do you know I don't think I will.'

Howard said lightly: 'Oh yes you will. It's leg-watching time.' He pushed the man firmly towards the railing that shut off the lower level.

'I say I say!' Domino exclaimed. 'This is all good stuff. You're running true to form. Jill's told me about your pad in Cavendish Street but she's got me a bit confused. I'm not sure if you're running a bookshop there, a gymnasium, or a school for naughty girls. "Strict discipline and personal attention. Brochure sent under plain cover. Wilful and difficult cases welcomed." That kind of thing. If that's the case I might pop along myself. In fact I'll bring my own cane.'

'Is Jill really here?' Howard asked. 'She said she wanted me to come to meet a few friends. Now I can't find her and there's this great mob.'

'Charming – oh very nice,' Domino said sarcastically. 'Poor darling then – won't I do as a substitute – even for a moment or two? She's over there but she's busy. Now don't be silly.'

Howard looked across the room following Domino's hand and saw Jill in a long green skirt and pale green high-necked blouse, talking animatedly to a man who wore a silver mask that completely covered his face and head.

'Use your barnet!' Domino said. She was no longer the heiress introduced to a member of the proletariat but her tone was impatient, as if Howard was now an obtuse pupil.

'Patience! Come downstairs but don't worry – I'm not suggesting you dance. There's a little game going on. A trial of strength. Should just suit you, speedy.'

They went downstairs and edged past the dancers to a door which Howard had not noticed, opening into a relatively small room. A heavily built man lay full length on the cream carpet, his body shaking with smothered laughter. There was a bottle in his outstretched hand and another lay by his side. Domino said, 'Up you get Fatty and let someone athletic try.' The man remonstrated mildly, saying something about 'my *amour propre*', but Domino ignored this and took the bottles away.

When the man had risen from the floor Domino showed Howard a line of paper napkins at the side of the room. 'Now you stand behind this. Supporting yourself on a bottle in each hand you see how far you can reach across the floor. You have to get right down flat of course. You stretch and put one bottle out as far as possible. Then with both hands holding the other bottle you have to move back behind the line. Without, needless to say, collapsing like a burst balloon. That's the record so far.' She pointed to a napkin about six feet or so from the line, then snatched off his Cyrano nose. 'You won't need this.'

Howard nodded. He was five feet ten inches in height. Someone like the thin tall youth would have the advantage in reaching out, but strength was more important because of the return journey, when the body had to be supported by both hands on the single bottle. He moved out and quickly reached the point where he could extend his left arm and place a bottle at least as far out as the marker. Now came the difficult part. With both hands clutching the neck of the other bottle, his body just arched above the floor, he jerked it back twice. As he was going to move it again he felt the gentle but firm pressure of a small foot on his neck. He tensed and resisted the foot's downward movement. He knew it was futile to do so: there was no more point in it than in the whole foolish game, but a physical challenge was something he found hard to resist. It was this kind of tenacity that had carried him through bouts with better and stronger boxers. The pressure was increased until his face was pressed down to touch the floor. He hung on for perhaps another thirty seconds, then collapsed as laughter broke out all round him.

He looked up to see a tall pale girl without a mask, wearing a turquoise trouser suit, looking down and smiling coolly at him. Under the bolero jacket she wore a cream silk shirt with a Byronic collar and long full sleeves. 'So you've given up eh? Ah well, nobody's perfect.'

When he was on his feet again she said, 'You can't win 'em all you know,' and then whispered in his ear: 'Strange but I have a certain penchant for weaklings. If one was to let slip a phone number could you be discreet?'

Howard was rescued from trying to reply to this with panache by Jill appearing in the doorway, removing her red domino, an unnatural smile set on her face as if it had been sewn on for the evening. She came towards him saying 'Oh hallo' in an off-hand way. The girl in the turquoise suit said, 'Are you going on to a certain place after?' with a significant shake of her head. Jill said 'No we're not' firmly, and the tall girl shrugged.

'Sorry, sorry, sorry – I'm sorry, darling' Jill murmured as they threaded their way past the dancers. 'Madness to rush you off like this but I must escape. *Now*.'

They went past the man in the silver mask, who watched them intently. Howard wondered if he was one of Jill's previous lovers. Jill's grip tightened on his wrist as though it was an encounter she dreaded, but nothing was said.

By the table laden with glasses she held Howard's right hand in both of hers. 'Won't be a jiff. Just got to get my coat.'

Howard waited by the door watching the lizard man who in turn was watching the girls dancing. The lizard's look was predatory and hungry. He surveyed the sensuously moving bodies as if he were selecting a live fish in a tank to be cooked for his dinner. Howard was perplexed at finding this un-abashed sexuality irritating when he was prey to similar moods. Affection, he thought, redeems it – otherwise what a cold, empty business it was, an oblation suitable for offering to the sand dollar god.

Jill took his hand again and they turned along the Greek blue corridor and then down the stairs. She showed her impatience when he looked for his coat on the glass table and as he opened the front door she broke into a run, tugging at his hand to make him go faster.

12

'Mm, it's nice to be home,' Jill said, taking the key from Howard's hand. She opened the lock without difficulty and gave him a charming little smile. He was thinking how different she was from the flippant girl who had knocked on the same door on Sunday night. She had not said a word walking back from Harley Street, lost in her own thoughts, holding his arm tightly. He was not going to press her about why she had asked him to the party, or why she had wanted to escape. When he had previously questioned her about her mode of living she had ended up by saying, 'I don't want to become your property, darling.' She was right in stressing that neither of them owned the other anything: it was a liaison only for today.

She paused on the mat, putting her arms round him. 'We are real friends – aren't we, Nick?' He smiled and kissed her. On the surface it was an absurd question to address to someone who had been her lover on the previous night but he knew what she meant. There was no doubt that he was growing very fond of her – he had realized how much when the lizard man had made that idly snide remark about her. He could not see what future their relationship could hold but he knew it would be hard to lose her. 'Friends for life,' he murmured with his face pressed into her hair. She pulled away, apparently unable to accept such a muzzy answer. 'No, tomorrow is just a guess,' she said, mirroring his thoughts.

She turned to stare out of the shop window, then moved to an angle that gave her a glimpse of the sky behind the Post Office tower. 'They said on the weather forecast that it would snow again. Well I hope it does, an absolute blizzard this time. Snow unendingly. Snow ten feet deep in New Cavendish Street – so that you have to get out of the window upstairs, using your tennis racquets as snow shoes to trudge to the delicatessen and the dairy. And I'll stop upstairs all the time ...' She shook her head as if to get rid of some unpleasant obtrusive thought.

When they were in the living-room Jill pushed Howard towards the couch. 'Now you sit quite still. I want to do everything tonight!' She slid the mat neatly into place over the trap-door, turned on a table-lamp, and extinguished the overhead one, then put on the Miles Davis Trio record of 'So What?' When she was curled up in his arms she said: 'Have you ever felt you were walking down a road without a turning? Do you know what I mean?'

'Indeed I do. I felt like that – just before I met you.'

'Really?' She gave a short bitter laugh.

'Yes, really.' He could see that she was troubled but was puzzled how to help her. 'What's wrong, Jill? Is it something you can tell me? I do wish you would say if it is.'

'Dear God, don't I wish I could. No, forget that. Mumbo-jumbo. Nothing at all. You know I'm a slap dash type person. A right mess in fact. So okay I must expect the occasional ballsups. Don't take any notice if I seem a trifle demented. It's – going – going – gone.'

She took off one mask only to reveal another. When he occasionally thought he glimpsed some genuine feeling, she was at pains to erase the impression. What an odd girl she was. He was twice her age, and her mind was like a rag-bag stuffed with unrelated facts and she had only the sketchiest possible knowledge of any subject, yet she was nearly always self-possessed while he was often awkward, floundering. It might be partly to do with belonging to different generations. Those girls still in their teens dancing at the party had as much self-assurance as professional performers; his generation tended to be less confident and more self-conscious. But beneath the surface confidence (what she called her 'flip exterior') he knew there was always something worrying Jill: a secret which lay between them like an invisible barrier that could not be surmounted.

On two occasions after making love to Jill, when he had lain with his head on her breast, feeling the quickened beat of her heart and smelling the balmy breath from her nostrils, he knew he had been very close to winning her confidence. Then the secret had appeared like a weighty object under water which could be lifted to a certain extent so that it shimmered just below the surface: and then, at exactly the moment when he expected to see it clearly, vanished.

Jill ran her index finger round his nails with a light tickling touch. 'Such moons! wasted on a man. Now – what I want is for us to be happy this evening and forget everything else. Okay? So are there enough buttons?' Her tone was breezy again.

'Enough?'

'Yes, you told me I would look nice in Edwardian clothes, "a high-necked blouse with lots of little mother-of-pearl buttons" which would be, I quote again, "delirium to undo".' She sat up in front of him. 'Would you call this a lot?'

'Enough.' He undid the buttons slowly, kissing her back each time another inch was revealed. When he had taken the blouse off he unfastened her brassiere and pressed his face into the hollow between her shoulder-blades, luxuriating in the warmth, the creamy texture of her skin and its smell mixed up with honeysuckle scent.

She moved forward from his embrace and stood up, turning round to face him as she took off her long green velvet skirt and white tights. She slipped down the lacy blue briefs through which her skin looked like ivory. All the time her eyes were fixed on his with an expression of loving tenderness. Free from her clothes she looked like a tree-nymph – so beautiful as to seem unapproachable.

'Up you get. Remember I'm in charge this evening.' With her eyes still on his she began to undo the buttons on his shirt while he kicked off his shoes. He held her waist and pulled her very gently towards him, delighting in the slight shock as her nipples touched his chest. Her breasts were as firm and explicitly rounded as nectarines. The smell of her body was as sweet as newly mown grass hot in the sun. He bent down to kiss her waist and the beginning curve of her belly.

She pulled him up. 'My turn, darling.' She ran her hands along his shoulders and down his arms. 'Barkis is willing,' she said, glancing down, and pushed him towards the couch. When he lay back she knelt before him, straddling his legs, moving forwards and backwards tantalizingly so that he could feel she was all liquid, then engulfed him.

Howard lay face down on a river bank, his arms outstretched, embracing the earth. The sun was warm on his back and the heat brought out the clover fragrance and another smell in the grass, sweet yet touched with an animal rankness like ground ivy. He looked up to see a heron taking off from a white post and flapping lazily away upstream.

With pedantic hesitations an enamel-backed beetle moved just in front of his face, picking its way between grass blades, like a cautious explorer in a jungle. A butterfly sunned itself on a stone, folding and opening its painted wings. High above a skylark was trilling away ceaselessly. For some moments Howard lay still, absorbed in watching the tiny water-boatman erratically skimming this way and that: then the river's surface suddenly turned black. Confronted by this opaque blackness which was at the same time a frightening void, Howard realized he was dreaming; he knew too that the pastoral scene was a prelude to terror, desperately wanted to wake up, and yet could not break away from the insidious embrace.

Slowly he got to his knees. The path took him through a profusion of budding meadow-sweet, loosestrife, and reeds. It was a familiar scene; a river-bank within sight of his house near Henley. Familiar but not exact – he wanted to protest about the topography of the dream – the path did not bend quite like this – there should be a copse on the opposite bank.

He parted a barrier of tall thistles and cow-parsley to begin climbing steps in a large building. It had some undefined clinical purpose – men and women in white clothes moved silently along the corridor's highly polished linoleum floor. It was in such a place as this that he had queued up to collect Meg's engagement and wedding rings on which he had found traces of blood.

Howard said 'This is only a dream', as though that was a talisman to protect him. He had passed through double doors and was in a hospital ward. Curtis Mahon lay on a bed, looking more like a large doll than a man, saying forbiddingly 'Of course if you want to play cheap chess with me.' There was confusion in Howard's mind whether this place was intended for bringing people back to life or putting them to death. A rubber-wheeled chrome trolley bore an axe as well as forceps. An amputated leg lay on a towel. Howard wanted to call out that he could not bear any more but no words would come. He was lost in a rich velvet cloud where a liquid manikin appeared and melted away over and over again. There was a roaring noise in his head as though life was departing.

I'm playing blind man's buff he thought, a dupe, a pawn with no control over his movements. The hospital beds and other surgical paraphernalia had been removed. Howard was in a court-room where Mahon as counsel was playing cat and mouse with his, saying 'Would it surprise you to know, Mr Howard?' He had no idea what the charge could be and yet struggled to think of some defence. He was so impressed by Mahon's protean personality that all he could do was foolishly repeat a chess rule he had learnt as a schoolboy: 'A King cannot be captured nor need it be removed from the board. It is enough that the King is put into a position from which it cannot escape.'

The desperate feeling of being duped and trapped vanished. Howard stood at the bottom of some narrow wooden stairs, holding his breath. Moonlight came in through an uncurtained window high on the left hand wall, otherwise the house was in darkness. He was naked and cold yet the palms of his hands were wet. He felt as though all his senses had been sharpened in some mysterious way: his touch as he ran his fingers over the banister was like that of a blind man sensitive to the minutest variations in the surface; he could hear the tiny scrabbling noises of birds in the roof gutters; his eyes detected every nuance of shadow. He moved up the stairs stealthily.

He entered a darkened bedroom, faintly discerning someone asleep, and approached to look down on a woman's body only partly covered by a sheet. Her head was pressed into a pillow. He put his hand down to feel the warmth of her breasts and then uncovered her legs. He knew there would be some terrible consequence in possessing her but nothing could stop him. He kissed her shadowy loins and parted her knees. The only thing in the world he wanted was to be lost in her unending embrace. 'Catherine,' he whispered.

As he moved forward the woman stirred from her sleep. It was Meg he held tight in his arms. It took all his strength to keep her by him for they stood on a cliff top and a merciless wind tugged at them while the sea pounded some hundred feet below. He struggled, but soon the weight of Meg's body was too much for him. Unavailing, he thought, as her shoulders were torn from his grasp. In desperation he grabbed her thin cold hands but they too slipped away and she fell, her mouth contorted in a silent scream.

For a moment Howard felt that he was falling too then woke from the dream, confused and unable to make sense of his surroundings. The position of his bed, the shadow of the wardrobe, the light reflected on the ceiling were all unfamiliar and disturbing. He sat up to see Jill was standing by the window, wearing his dressing-gown. With a sigh of relief he threw off the nightmare's jumbled images. Jill's profile was outlined by lights in the street below and seen like that she looked even younger and touchingly beautiful. Large flakes of snow were drifting down and some of them melted on the window. Absorbed and pensive, Jill appeared remote from her surroundings like the child in the fairy story about the Snow Queen: Howard remained still, careful not to disturb her until he saw that she was brushing away some tears. Then he sprang out of bed and put his arms round her shoulders, trying to comfort her, but large tears continued to well up silently. On several occasions he had found her behaviour enigmatic, but he was completely baffled by her crying.

'Darling Jill – don't. What's wrong? You must tell me. I can't bear to see you cry.' He pulled her tentatively towards the bed as she made a slight whimpering noise. 'Please, please, tell me.' She shook her head and stared out again at the snow being blown this way and that. It was as if she had retreated far into herself like an injured cat.

Howard touched her hands. 'You're cold. Shivering.' He bent down and carried her to the bed, tucking her up like a child. He switched on the bedside lamp and crouched on the floor, putting his right arm loosely across the eiderdown. She remained mute but pushed both hands out of the bedclothes and made an odd little movement with her index fingers as if she were knitting, looking at him with eyes still wet with tears.

'There may be something I can do, Jill. Do talk to me. It's terrible seeing you like this – you were so happy earlier. What's gone wrong?'

There was a long pregnant silence. Something about her expression made him realize that she was at last on the verge of telling him her secret.

'Are you . . .?' She made the brief knitting motion again. 'Are you all tangled up with me, Nick?'

'Do you mean do I care for you? Of course I do. You little fool, you know that. You can't be crying about that.'

Jill sighed deeply then said: 'Turn out the light, darling. It will be easier to talk in the dark. Get into bed and I'll try to explain.'

When he was lying close and holding her hands she said, 'This is going to hurt you, darling. Badly, I think. It's oh such a

118

hopeless mess. I simply dread telling you but there's no other way out. Will you promise me not to do anything about what I say for at least a day? Other people are involved, friends I knew long before you – and it's complicated by lots of things. Will you swear to keep it to yourself until I've had a chance to see them?'

'I'll do whatever you want. You know that.'

'Ah, you say that now. But you'll feel differently when I tell you. So promise me?' She pulled his right hand over her breast so that he could feel her pounding heart.

'Yes, I promise.' Long-seeming minutes passed in silence again – so many that he wondered if she was going to say anything more.

She spoke very quietly: 'That night we met. It – it wasn't by accident. I planned to meet you somehow, to pick you up.'

Howard felt that this might be emotional nonsense. He had become used to Mcg's rare but disturbing menstrual moods when she would say similarly wild things. 'But that's absurd. You didn't pick me up. You were being sick, remember? I came up to you by that statue...'

She turned to him with an unhappy smile, shaking her head. 'It's true, darling. I was told to pick you up. The sick – it just happened. You see I was waiting about for a long while, first of all for you to come out from here, and I popped into that pub opposite for a drink or two. The drinks on an empty stomach, being cold hanging around in the snow, feeling nervous following you. That made me sick. But if you hadn't come up then I should have found some way of meeting you.'

It was Howard's turn to feel slightly sick. Her confession had the ring of truth. He was mystified about the reason for her deception but he could not protest it again. It was deflating to find out that his attraction for her had been non-existent, though he had always been slightly suspicious about it: the mystery behind this plot was much more disturbing. Unformulated doubts and fears which had previously hovered about him, only finding expression in his confused dream, began to make more sense. Being conned by Jill – that explained his presentiment of being manipulated, moved like a pawn in a game of chess.

'But why?' he asked in a voice devoid of expression. His hand was still on her breast but he felt drained of sexual and emotional feelings, cold and detached.

She sensed his changed attitude and pressed his hand even tighter against her. 'Don't hate me now, Nick. I care for you – we're friends – it's because I'm fond of you I had to tell you.'

'Then tell me why.'

'Some people I know – they wanted me to do it. It was a rotten trick – so okay I've been unhappy and I've done some very dodgy things. I told you my life was in a mess. They wanted you to get tangled up with me so that I could tell them about what you were doing and . . .'

'You mean some kind of blackmail. If I got "tangled up" I should be willing to do something for them?' A thought struck him suddenly. 'That first night when I went to your flat. There was a man waiting in the street when I came out. I suppose he was there on purpose – for the blackmail. A big man with owl-like eyes. Is he one of your friends?'

'No, I don't know him. But I once heard they had employed a man who fits that description. He's a kind of detective, runs a small private agency off Oxford Street. They used him to keep someone quiet. But what they want with you . . . I simply can't understand it . . .'

'I think I can.' Some part of Howard's mind had been occupied in ransacking memory files: he thought of the page of notes he had taken from Bina Gardens. 'Yes, it must be something to do with Nancy Douce, that West Indian girl I mentioned. The house where we went this evening, it's called Park Place isn't it?' Finished with rifling memories, a queer sort of logic was emerging. 'Did they ask you to bring me along there so they could see what kind of a fool they were dealing with? That man in the silver mask. Is his name Paton?'

'No.' Her false emphasis told Howard that she was lying. Probably she feared that he would not give her the day's grace she wanted, that he would go straight round to Park Place and question Paton.

She turned round to look at him closely. 'Please do understand, Nick. I told them tonight that I wasn't going on with this rotten business and there was a hell of a row. It's something very serious. They're frightened and that's frightened me. But if you give me a day perhaps I can find out what's at the bottom of it. If you still care for me at all don't do anything till then. You see ...' She made a hopeless gesture. 'I'm mixed up with them.'

'Yes, I do see.' Howard said this coldly and they relapsed into an uneasy silence. When she realized he was not going to ask any more questions Jill curled up into the foetus-like posture she adopted for sleeping, but he lay with his eyes wide open, staring at the ceiling, knowing that he would remain awake for the rest of the night. He held Jill's hand for perhaps half an hour until she relaxed her anxious grip and he could tell from her breathing that she had found the refuge from reality she desired, then got up and went into the living-room.

When he tried to understand the mysterious affair in which he was apparently involved, the image of a game of chess struck him as being most appropriate. After Nancy Douce vanishes, Nicholas Howard goes to her lodgings. Someone else also visits Bina Gardens to see what inquiries have been made about Nancy and reports to X (Larry Paton?) that Howard had been there. Howard's connection with Nancy is tenuous, but X being in the dark to the extent of knowing very little about Howard decides that counter moves must be made just in case he should give trouble. Howard was struck by a bitter thought: how exactly X had taken his measure! Howard? – a vain man of early middle-age anxious to be reassured that women find him attractive – a young beautiful girl as a decoy was the simple answer.

13

The single diesel moved slowly out from Twyford station round the curving branch line to Henley. When it had gathered speed its moving lights, together with sparks from the frosted rails, fitfully illuminating the snow-covered fields, gave the humdrum landscape a touch of magic. Howard stared out of the train window noting the bizarre appearance of hedges and trees he had seen a hundred times. Nothing appeared quite as usual on this routine journey, but he realized it was probably due to his own nervous state of mind. The events of the day since Jill had gone off to make her inquiries had led him farther into a maze, and he felt sure that the way out would only be found by making unhappy discoveries. He had kept his promise to Jill but had not allowed it to divert him from taking up Nancy's disappearance with the police as Carew's cable had requested.

At Marylebone Lane Police Station a uniformed sergeant from D Division had helped him to fill in Form 584A for Missing Persons. When this had been completed he had been asked to wait, and then the alert-looking sergeant returned to suggest that Howard went to West End Central Station 'to give more information'.

As he was whisked in a white Jaguar down New Bond Street to the large Savile Row building, Howard was thinking hard about his opposing allegiances to Jill Lammas and Mrs Nina Douce. He decided he would tell the police about Nancy's notes which he had found at Bina Gardens without giving his reasons for now finding them to be so significant.

Seated in a cubicle-like office in the West End Central Station in which there was just room for three chairs and the kind of a desk a schoolboy might use for his homework, Howard had found he needed to keep his wits about him. Questions were put to him by a cheerful man who appeared to be much too young to be a detective inspector. The third chair, in the corner of the room, was occupied by an older man who seemed not to be concerned with the interview, smoking a cigarette and reading a Racing Edition of the *Evening Standard* which was spread out on the floor.

Inspector Wishart had taken Howard at a fast clip through the information he had already given on the form and then asked him to supplement the details listed under the headings 'Habits and mode of life' and 'Circumstances under which missing'. Wishart combined an easy manner with an air of concentration, which gave Howard the impression that each of his sentences was being taken away and tested for reliability.

Wishart's casual approach, a sorry-about-all-these-formalities attitude, only wavered once – when Howard spoke of his belief that the police were already involved because of what the

Pattersons had said at Bina Gardens. At this point Wishart glanced at the third man as if for guidance but none was forth-coming.

While Wishart studied Mrs Douce's letter and the notes found at Nancy's lodgings, Howard felt guilty about suppress-ing a comment which might be vital and began to long for the interview to be over. Its termination was apparently signalled by a cough from the older man and the *Evening Standard* being folded up clumsily. As Howard left the small office the third man nodded at him as if acknowledging his existence for the first time.

The train shuddered as it crossed the Thames just after stop-ping at Wargrave. The river, swollen and fast-running, looked particularly dark and mysterious as it swirled between snow-covered banks. Viewed from the river, as he had so often seen it, the single coach and the old-fashioned bridge would resemble a child's train set. And in the miniature train the doll-like pass-engers, himself included, obsessed with their little hopes, desires and fears. Seen like that, what a trifling matter anyone's life appeared. For a moment the people he had met in the last few days, Curtis Mahon, Quincy Adams, Mrs Douce, Jill, Edith Voysey, whirled round in Howard's head. He saw Miss Voysey keeping her top lip still to hide her denture, Mrs Douce's trem-bling hands, Jill's eyes brimming with tears, and was over-whelmed by the pathos and transience of human lives – people seemed as ephemeral as mayflies or midges which would hover for a while above the river on a summer day.

When the train stopped at Shiplake Howard opened his brief-case. He intended to spend the night at his house near Henley, so he had brought some cheese and biscuits and a tin of instant coffee. Also in the case there were four pages of shorthand notes apparently written by Nancy which he had found in her copy of *The Magus*. When he had returned in the afternoon to New Cavendish Street from the house auction at Knightsbridge, he had picked up *The Magus* idly thinking he might read it that evening. Inside the front cover there were the thin pages of copy yping paper, effectively concealed when the large book was osed.

The shorthand notes were prefaced by a few sentences in

Nancy's handwriting – these appeared to be extracts from an old book on Ghosts:

> It should have been observed that Ghosts,
> in delivering their commiffions, in order
> to ensure belief, communicate to the perfons
> employed fome fecret, known only to the
> parties concerned and themfelves, the relation
> of which always produces the effect intended . . .

> The mode of addreffing a Ghoft is by commanding it, in the
> name of the Three Perfons of the Trinity, to tell you who
> it is and what is its bufiness . . .

At the end of the war, hoping to alleviate the boredom of idle months in Hamburg, Howard had begun a correspondence course in shorthand with the intention of taking a job as a journalist after he had been demobilized. But the lack of concentration which had prevented him from mastering chess had soon led to the Pitman's books being buried in his kitbag. Now, looking at Nancy's shorthand notes, he found he could only pick out the odd word. This was frustrating but he knew the riddle could be solved easily the following day, and if it proved to be of any consequence could then be handed to the police. What to do about Jill's further revelations, which he was expecting to receive later that evening by phone, was a more difficult problem.

He pondered this as the train made its brisk approach to Henley, then forgot it in thoughts of Meg. He had made this journey on numerous occasions in the past twenty years as he found it more convenient than travelling to London by car, with all the attendant problems of parking, but this was the first time that Meg would not be there to meet him.

The spry old man who drove the hired car was keen to talk, but after commenting on the council's tardiness in dealing with icy road conditions he was off on his hobby-horse about how things in general had got worse, and Howard was able to think his own thoughts, only adding an occasional yes or a grunt of agreement.

When they passed his old shop in Bell Street, empty exce

for a To Let sign propped up in the front window, Howard felt a sharp pang of longing for his life as it had been only a few months before. Meg popping into the shop to see if there was anything she could do to help; going off together to auction sales in Devon or Dorset, returning with the car piled high with books. He realized now that she was the only person who had ever really cared for him – to Catherine Gurney he had been a divertissement during a dull winter – to Jill Lammas he had been a curious assignment. Yet when life had been normal he had become bored. Was this perverse state of affairs inevitable with human beings or just a sign of shallowness in his own character?

'Sand? Yes, all right, if they get the beggars out early enough to tackle the job and clear it away after. But putting down this salt? Madness. Horrid muck – just rusts your chassis You really need to hose down that car after each trip and of course you can't do that ...' The old man had apparently got back to the difficulties of driving in winter.

Howard nodded his agreement as he got out of the car. It was a particularly clear night without a single cloud. 'No more snow tonight anyway,' he said as he paid the driver. 'Freezing hard.'

Howard paused before opening the front gate. Going back alone into the house where he had lived with Meg for nearly twenty years took some resolution. But he had made up his mind to tackle several other jobs on this trip apart from looking out the clothes Jacqueline wanted. At last he was going to face up to making a list of pieces of furniture to be put into store and others to be sold; he would also sort out odds and ends he was going to bundle up for Oxfam, and tidy things up generally.

Howard walked across the lawn which was so rigidly frozen that it was like treading on stone, and bent down to look at the clump of snowdrops which grew under the hedge. An owl was calling from the holly-tree. The first buds of honeysuckle would just be appearing. Strange to think that by the time daffodils bloomed the house might be sold and another family living there. For a moment he looked across the field to the bend of the river he had revisited in his nightmare, then steeled himself to enter the house.

Once inside it was not as bad as he had feared. There was a fire set in the sitting-room grate and he lit this straight away, then brought down Jacqueline's transistor set so that he could listen to some music. He intended to sleep downstairs on the couch so he took blankets from a cupboard to air before the fire. Being in the army for five years had induced a discipline about making oneself reasonably comfortable; and keeping busy, doing one job after another, was essential.

He was upstairs taking some clothes from Jacqueline's wardrobe when the phone rang. Without thinking he answered it in the main bedroom, now practically bare of furniture. As he picked up the receiver from the floorboards he caught sight of his face in the dressing-table mirror and visualized Meg sitting in front of it, talking to his mirrored image as she did her hair.

There was a pause and then the operator asked if he would accept a reversed charge call from a London phone box, from a Miss Jill Lammas. There was another delay after he said yes, and Jill's voice began confusingly half-way through some explanation about not having enough change. He interrupted her impatiently to say 'It doesn't matter', though he understood she had said it only because she was loath to get to the point.

There was another silence and he imagined her looking about wildly as she did occasionally when at a loss for words. When she did speak she sounded terribly nervous. 'I know you'll be angry but I want more time. I haven't been able to find the girl I was looking for. Give me another day, please, Nick.'

'Do you mean you've been looking for Nancy Douce?'

'No – I wouldn't have a clue where to begin with her, but I do know a girl who may know what happened ... She seems to have gone into hiding too ...'

'Is it Larry Paton who's behind this business? You must tell me that.'

She hesitated, began a sentence as if she was going to deny it again, then changed her mind. 'He's mixed up in it,' she agreed grudgingly. 'But it's more complicated than that. I'm afraid it's something terrible but Larry's only on the fringe. Another day and I'll find out for certain.'

'All right. I shall be coming back to London tomorrow, in the afternoon I expect. Leave a message for me at Cavendish Street or phone me there in the evening.' He found it impossible to put any feeling into his words; he realized he did not want to see her again.

'Yes, yes, I'll do that. But don't ring off yet – there's something else. You must be fed up with me, even hate me – but I am trying to help now. That man you mentioned seeing in Pimlico, near my flat. I'm positive he is the private detective I'd heard about. His name is Gallacher, Monk Gallacher. He's got a nasty reputation as being a kind of professional frightener. I think this crowd I know have got him watching you – it seems they're scared about something you know or something you might find out. It's ...' She hesitated, as if these last words were being wrung out of her. 'I think it may be connected with your wife in some way.'

Howard had intended to ask her how Gallacher could be watching him at the moment unless she had divulged his intention to go to Henley and Hambleden Mill, but this was put out of mind once she mentioned Meg. It was like being brushed by the wing of a strange nightmarish bird: bewilderment and unreasoning fear held him so confused that he did not know what to say for a minute. When he did speak his voice was uncertain and shaky: 'But how could she be involved? I just don't understand.'

'I don't either – unless she knew or guessed something about Nancy Douce ...' Jill made a gulping noise and Howard knew she was crying. 'I'm so frightened, Nick. You see I think Nancy Douce may be dead.' The line clicked without her saying goodbye and for a minute Howard waited expecting she might speak again.

When he did replace the mute receiver Howard remained where he was, staring out of the window with unseeing eyes. Poor little Nancy Douce. Now that it had been expressed, Jill's verdict on Nancy had authority and seemed irrevocable – because, he realized, it expressed his own subconscious thoughts. Once his inquiry at Marylebone Lane Police Station had begun to receive special treatment he had been suspicious. That subtle interview at Savile Row was obviously not standard procedure for anyone who came in to report a missing person.

Poor Nancy. And Meg – how could she have been mixed up in this affair? He began to visualize a possible sequence of events. Nancy had vanished on December 14th. If Meg had been informed about Nancy's London friends it was possible that she had asked them awkward questions. Those weeks when Meg had been so moody – for all he knew it was possibly because she had gone to one of the parties at Park Place, and was unhappy about Nancy becoming more involved with Larry Paton and his friends. Then, if Meg had pressed on with her inquiries, perhaps threatened to go to the police? Fear made Howard's heart leap. The man old Mrs Voysey had seen rushing out on to the platform at Oxford Circus, catching Meg off balance – had that really been an accident? He cursed his stupidity for not seeing this before, and then accepted it was guilt and not stupidity that had blinded him. For weeks he'd been punchdrunk with guilt and remorse. When the police had talked to him about Meg's death, his main concern had been in case they probed into his life and discovered the liaison with Catherine Gurney.

Howard opened the window and leaned out, looking up above the bare elm branches at the stars. His reverie was broken by a small noise on the gravel path immediately below. He looked down to see the big man with owl-like eyes. Gallacher wore a dark blue or black monkey jacket with his hands thrust deep in the pockets, lounging with a casual air as though he was waiting there legitimately. He grinned until Howard called out 'Gallacher, I want you', then his face showed he was surprised or disconcerted at his name being known. He said nothing but his expression became scornful. After staring thoughtfully at Howard for a moment he turned and ran down the path to the gate.

Howard tore down the stairs and chased out after the big man, who ran along the road with a lightness of step that was surprising for someone so heavily built. Howard had expected to see Gallacher running towards a parked car but instead he turned down the drive that led to the mill and the river.

Howard sprinted round the mill buildings confident that he would catch up with him on the path there, but found it was empty, which meant that Gallacher must have begun to run faster still. At the end of the fence Howard saw the big man

waiting for him, standing some fifty feet or so along the concrete cat-walk over the system of weirs and flood-gates which
spanned the river at its widest point. Gallacher gripped the
metal rails on either side and held himself suspended in the air,
moving his feet backwards and forwards like a boy playing. The
wind blowing across from the fields on the other side of the
Thames was bitterly cold and when Howard stopped running
he shivered.

The big man was grinning widely again as though he welcomed the confrontation, confident things would go just as he
dictated. Howard had been knocked round the ring by too many
boxers with a similar weight and reach advantage to be optimistic if they tangled, but he did not intend to turn back.

Gallacher spoke tauntingly: 'Come and try your luck, Tich.'
Being slightly out of breath made his voice lugubrious - as if it
had been recorded at 78 r.p.m. and was being played at 33.
There was no jokey Australian accent this time. He moved his
heavy shoulders and then held up his fists with the backs turned
towards Howard as if to show him their size. 'I may take pity
on you. You never know. On the other hand I may just flatten
you.'

Howard said calmly: 'I wanted to ask you about my wife.
Was it you who pushed her on to the line? I shall find out you
know and you'll get more than a fist sandwich then.'

'Your wife?' Gallacher appeared momentarily disconcerted
again. 'I've never seen her.' He paused and then his tone became
blustering: 'Unless you mean that cheap little tart you've been
shacked up with in New Cavendish Street. That black-haired
whore. Now I know a lot about her. And you of course. What a
cosy two-some. Oh what a f—ing fool you were about her. But
then, I mean, well you're not too bright are you? Why do you
think I ran away from your house? Because I was scared of
you? You mug, I wanted to get you somewhere quiet. Nice spot
like this where I can give you some homework and we won't be
disturbed.' He had a deep laugh with a rasp in it.

Howard said: 'This isn't a chat so you can cut out the
patter.'

Gallacher smiled knowingly. 'Oh – well I thought it *could* be
ıst a chat. Up to you of course. A nice little chat to remind

you, Mr Butt-insky, that you've been mixed up with a right young tart who's known to the police. What a nasty story it will make and we've got photographs to prove it. But perhaps you'd prefer to have the warning?'

Howard thought this sounded like a prepared statement being read out after having been made meaningless by the turn of events. Gallacher was like one of those Japanese soldiers on atolls in the Pacific who did not know when the war was over. It would be sensible to put him in the picture, to tell him that Detective Inspector Wishart and his grey-haired, thoughtful colleague were taking a great interest in all matters concerning Nancy Douce and her friends. It would be sensible to turn tail and race back along the cat-walk. It would be sensible to do anything apart from further provoking this 'professional frightener', but he was not in the mood to be sensible.

Gallacher seemed to have run out of dialogue. Obviously he was only equipped with a few lines and he had got tired of them; his everted lips were fixed in a sneering smile. Howard was sizing up his opponent. In an inter-services boxing tournament he had once fought a Scottish aircraftsman just as big and strong as Gallacher, so he knew how much of a problem he faced. And in that long ago bout he had a boxing-ring to back-pedal in, whereas the cat-walk gave no room for manoeuvre.

Gallacher's gross features were now set like a mask, but the impassiveness could not altogether disguise the pleasure he found in his present situation; he was a man who had become used to hurting people and found he had a taste for it. He tauntingly jigged about in front of Howard, displaying his surprising agility: he feinted with his left fist and hit Howard with a right cross. Howard side-stepped at the right second so that the blow did not connect with his face, but it grazed his collar-bone and ear with jolting power. As the big man moved forward, carried along by the momentum of punching his full weight, Howard rocked him with a left jab. His jab wasn't as good as Henry Cooper's but it was his best punch.

Gallacher's head snapped back and he moved away, shaking his head to clear it, re-appraising the situation. It appeared that he had decided to dispense with the boxing lesson because he charged forward like a bull, ignoring two more jabs. Howar stepped back but slipped on a patch of ice, falling forward into Gallacher's arms which fastened round him like a pinion. As Howard strained backwards Gallacher brought his knee up into Howard's groin. The pain of this was so intense that Howard collapsed writhing on the concrete path. His vision was covered by a kind of inky mucilage: someone seemed to be screaming inside his head. Everything reeled about him. He was only partly aware of Gallacher bending down to seize his feet and push him like a wheel-barrow over the side of the cat-walk into the river.

The shock of entering the icy water after the intense pain in his groin took Howard's breath away; he became as limp as though he had given up hope and was content to drown. He was only dimly aware of being borne along by the torrent and of his face being hit with great concentrated splashes; it was as if someone was throwing buckets of water at him with the intention of forcing open his mouth. It all seemed to be happening to a third person. Somebody else was surviving this.

At the edge of the weir's boiling movement of water the straight-forward current was so strong that it too had an unreal quality, like effortless motion in a dream. When it slowed he was forced down head-first and he felt that he lacked the strength to get back to the surface, just concentrating on covering his mouth and nose with his hands. Once he bobbed up the nightmarish nature of his ordeal vanished: he could see that he had been swirled into a relatively calm backwater near the left-hand bank going downstream to Marlow. The pain in his groin was ebbing but the numbing coldness of the water threatened to sap his strength before he could get to shore. Floating on his back he managed to kick off his moccasin shoes, and then struggled feebly to undo his jacket. He found that it was impossible to take it off, and he swam with slow breast-strokes as though tangled up in a weighted net.

He got up on his knees and then collapsed again in the shallow water at the river's edge, dragging himself out by scrabbling in the mud and ice-covered reeds. Then he lay face down on the bank, exhausted, quite unable to move, not caring about anything. Complete consciousness ebbed back slowly till he could hear the distant roar of water through the flood-gates and the wind moaning in the trees. When at last he managed to clamber to his feet, he stood shivering with exaggerated movements, his teeth chattering uncontrollably.

Making his way back along the bank to the mill buildings he felt like a patient who had been bed-ridden for months learning how to use his legs again: each step took a conscious effort of will. His ribs ached and his breath came in painful spasms. He stood still for a few moments searching the area for Gallacher, then heard a car's starter and saw headlights on the road to Marlow.

By the time he reached his garden muddy water was only trickling down his legs, but he tore off his remaining clothes at the front door. A big rather ragged towel remained in the bathroom cupboard and he used this vigorously to bring back life first into his hands and then his legs. He caught sight of himself in the mirror as he towelled his behind. His hair was plastered to his scalp with mud, his body grey and purple in patches. His phallus, which Jill had called 'Barkis', was shrivelled and puny, looking as if it would never be 'willing' again. It was hard to imagine anyone more abject and bedraggled. How easily a body was stripped of dignity and made absurd. But not feelings: they were not falsely dignified. He looked down at himself again. Absurd clown-figure he thought – and yet he did not regret his futile effort to stand up to Gallacher.

As he walked into the living-room warmth came surging back to his body. He pushed the couch nearer to the fire and drank half a tumbler of sherry, then piled blankets on the couch like a somnambulist. His last thought was: Round One to Monk Gallacher and I'll let Inspector Wishart take him on in Round Two. He crawled between the blankets, an animal going into hibernation, and fell into a dreamless sleep.

14

Nicholas Howard sat in a taxi going along George Street, feeling like a piece of old and very fragile porcelain; for the fifth or sixth time he gingerly touched his shoulders and tracked down particularly tender spots. He had returned to Paddington approximately twenty-four hours after leaving it on his way to Henley. He had been so exhausted by the evening's entertainment devised by Monk Gallacher that he had slept through till noon and then had moved round the house at a cripple's pace, doing about half of the jobs he had intended to accomplish. Every muscle in his body ached and he was covered with small bruises and scratches which he had not noticed in the previous examination in the mirror. The only injury that might be serious was the one made by Gallacher's knee, which had left a dramatically coloured bruise extending its yellow rim across his navel.

At Henley he had bought a tin of plasters and retired to a public lavatory to stick them on, then enjoyed a meal which had served as breakfast, lunch, and tea. He had phoned his assistant at the bookshop to say he would be back before closing time, but he was arriving back later than that. He could blame his tardy return on sitting too long over the meal, but really it was dictated by his reluctance to face up to all that awaited him – the phone-call that Jill would make and the action he would have to take on hearing her revelations.

The taxi dropped him where George Street met Marylebone High Street. It was 7.15 p.m. and his assistant would have given up expecting him and gone home. Perhaps Jill's message would be waiting, duly recorded on the dreaded telephone answering machine. As he walked up New Cavendish Street towards his shop he saw a familiar car parked in Westmoreland Street by the Duke of York pub. It was the yellow Mini-Cooper with the 'psychedelic' coloured chicken on its door which had transported Jill on the Sunday evening he had returned from Grenada. It had only one occupant, a youth in an old-fashioned black coat and black hat with a floppy brim, who got out as soon as he saw Howard and raced across the street.

'At last!' the youth exclaimed. 'I've been waiting there for about an hour. Jill wants to see you. It's urgent. Something's wrong with her, poor kid. It's a bad scene I'm afraid.' He looked questioningly at Howard as though he might be in part to blame. Despite the youth's floppy hat, lace-fronted shirt, and bizarre long black jacket which could have been worn by a sheriff in a silent cowboy film, there was no doubt about his masculinity. He gave Howard a searching look with keen grey eyes when there was no reply to his statement.

Howard sighed. He did not relish another interview with Jill; he had hoped the tedious business could be done by a phone call. 'Where is she then?'

The youth shook his head. 'I don't know exactly. She's had some trouble at her place in Pimlico and cleared out. And she doesn't want to come here. So she asked me to transport you to a house in Chelsea.' He glanced down at his watch. 'We ought to be off now.'

'Okay.' Howard got into the Mini with what must have appeared exaggerated care. It struck him that this was what it would be like to be old and arthritic, judiciously lifting one's legs into place, trying to minimize jolts of pain.

The youth gave him another long look while the elaborate seating ritual was taking place, then sped off. Howard had never travelled so fast in London before: the youth gripped the red wheel, showing knuckles that looked as if they had been through a wind screen, and they shot along Oxford Street and down Park Lane, overtaking every car in sight, going past lights when they were amber, and turning red, cutting all the corners. The risks that the youth took continually did at least keep Howard from thinking about what was to follow when he met Jill. The Mini shot down Sloane Street, mysteriously eluding a dozen possible crashes, gave an old lady on a pedestrian crossing a taste of terror, then abruptly braked in the Royal Hospital area. When the journey ended Howard did not know whether to congratulate the driver or say a prayer.

The youth nipped out and ran round to open Howard's door for him, suspecting that the unloading procedure might be as lengthy as the seating. Howard got out as quickly as possible, ignoring a sharp twinge of pain, and followed the youth up a short path to a handsome Georgian house.

The door was opened by a raffish middle-aged man who was dressed to look younger in over-tight cord trousers and a mid-blue mohair pullover with a scarf tied at the neck. The man did not bother to disguise his disappointment at seeing who had rung the bell. The youth said: 'This is Mr Howard. He's a friend of Jill Lammas. She'll be here shortly,' and walked off.

The man frowned then gave Howard a weak smile, and they went down a hall-way so discreetly lit that it was impossible to tell if the paper on the wall was dark green or dark blue. Joss-sticks were being burnt. A room on the right was full of people circulating round a large table loaded with food. There was not so much evidence of champagne as there had been at Park Place but more variety of things to eat, including several large dishes containing rich-looking sweets. The man who had let Howard in said: 'Will you help yourself? You can see it's rather a whirl.'

A youth with a contrived startled fawn expression in a dainty outfit of beige cowboy shirt, skin-tight pants, and high black shiny boots sidled up to Howard holding out a bowl he had filled with his own hands. 'Lover, try the rose cream. It's the authentic Paul Reboux recipe. Made with essence of *la rose Jacqueminot*.' It seemed a disinterested action on his part, or else he did not warm to Howard at close quarters, because he turned away once the bowl was accepted.

Someone who had been watching this sally said 'Whose the Poof-in-Boots?' but Howard did not catch the reply as there was a scented whisper in his ear: 'Give me chastity and continency but do not give it yet.' He looked round to see the tall blonde girl who had trodden on his neck at Park Place. She stuck a finger-tip in his rose cream and licked it with a cat-like tongue. 'St Augustine,' she added, to give the source of the quotation. 'No wonder you're not very strong if you're always sponging up stuff like this.' She ran a hand over his stomach, not realizing she was giving him pain rather than pleasure, then explored his trouser front. 'Do you . . .' She looked at him with eyes as innocent as if they were shaking hands. 'Come here often?' Howard shook his head, out-paced by all this smart stuff. It's pipe-and-slippers-time for me he thought. A corner seat by the fire.

'Haven't you finished stuffing yet for God's sake?' she inquired with mock irritation, dragging him out of the room. 'Here's a fun something.' She opened a door on the left to disclose a room lit by an ultra-violet bulb. Once his eyes were accustomed to the unusual light, Howard saw that the room contained only an extremely large bed. There was a mirror on the ceiling and another very large one on the wall such as ballet dancers use in practising. The tall girl pushed him towards this. 'Say aren't you the dark meat though. I don't know about the bed bit now seein' you all like this 'cos I's strictly a Southern girl at heart.'

In the mirror Howard did indeed look like a Negro, but all in all it was a flattering reflection, making his teeth appear whiter than in reality and toning up the skin. It was quite a tonic after the image in the mirror at Henley. His companion gave a melon-eating grin. 'One really can't have too much of this sort of thing. I mean to see oneself as one knows, in one's heart of hearts, one really is.' Howard grinned back at her.

She held his hand tightly and said, 'Easy, baby. This ...' – she indicated the bed – 'is the savoury course. First you need the aperitif.' Going into the passage again they turned left towards the back of the house and came to a glass door leading into a large room which was in darkness apart from the erratic illumination of a film being shown on a screen set against curtained french windows. It was a silent melodrama to which facetious sub-titles had been added in white painted script. The heroine was warding off the villain and underneath the joker had written: 'Not today, Jack. Isn't it a Curse?'

Howard's attention was distracted from the closing scenes of the old film by the raffish man in cord trousers who was fondling the breasts of a young girl standing in front of him. This attention did not appear to be welcome and the young girl was trying to pull away. Howard turned to the tall blonde but she had vanished, her place being taken by 'Poof-in-Boots' who was saying to a short fat man: 'Actually I'm not much of a brawler, more of a dancer really.'

Me too, mate, thought Howard. He wanted to escape from this house: he did not like the paraphernalia assembled in the various rooms, nor the hot-house atmosphere of burning joss-sticks and self-conscious eroticism. The silent film had stopped flickering and was replaced by one of rather more recent date, of the sylvan 'blue' variety. A nude young man, whose eyes seemed to signal that his true interests lay elsewhere, discovered a partly clothed girl asleep in a woodland glade. Howard was uneasy at the audience's rapt silence when the actors began to copulate and at the way they were being manipulated, like marionettes dangling from the hand of an unseen giant, as they were being prepared for the 'savoury'.

Leaving the darkened room he spied the tall girl peering at a book which she promptly held out, saying: 'Now this is quite something. Would you believe *Yvonne or the Adventures and Intrigues of a French Governess with her Pupils ...*? By Mary Suckit? Honest.'

Everything in the place was directed to one end, like a slaughter-house, and it was depressing Howard – he remembered a line from Edmond de Goncourt's *Journal* 'Debauchery is perhaps an act of despair in the face of infinity.'

Over the blonde's shoulder Howard saw with relief that the mysterious black-garbed youth had appeared again, standing in the open doorway. Howard looked at his attractive companion who was reading out a passage from *Yvonne* and felt that for a moment he had an insight into her profound boredom and emptiness. 'I'm afraid I've got to go,' he said as the youth beckoned.

'Oh, not yet. It may have been a little Dullsville so far but it's liable to get quite frisky later on.'

'I bet,' said Howard, making for the door. He was hoping that the youth being by himself did not mean that they were going off again in the Mini, but once they were outside the boy pointed along the Embankment, saying, 'Jill's waiting for you – on the bridge. Very upset, so try to cheer her up if you can.'

When Howard reached Ranelagh Gardens he could see Jill walking to and fro on Chelsea Bridge rather like a mechanical doll, taking a dozen steps in one direction then turning back. As he got nearer he saw that she carried a small attache case in her right hand; the limp tiger cub he had given her dangled from her left. Hearing his footsteps she stood still, listlessly looking towards Battersea Park. Her physical attraction for him had not diminished in the least and he knew it would be a long time before he would be able to forget her. He put his hand on her arm: 'Well, Jill? What did you find out?'

She did not reply but made a gulping, snuffling noise, holding her face rather stiffly so that he could only see one side. He took her head in both hands and very gently turned it towards him. She was not crying but the gulping noises were the aftermath of a prolonged bout of sobbing. Her aquamarine eyes, with their child-like clearness, framed by wet lashes, were touchingly beautiful. She had made a fool of him, spied on him, told him lies, but he had been wrong to think that he was no longer tangled up with her. 'What's wrong, dear girl?'

She sniffed twice, then got out two rather choky sentences: 'That nasty joker I told you about – Gallacher – paid me a visit. Smashed up my flat and knocked me down.' She raised the hand holding the tiger cub so that he could see a dark bruise circling her wrist like a bracelet. Howard had never hated anyone in his life: he did not hate Gallacher but he promised himself that he would be diligent in seeing some retribution was forthcoming.

He was unable to say anything but Jill could see that he was upset: 'Oh, it's not serious, Nick. And my stuff, you've seen it, there's nothing valuable. It was just coming on top of everything else.'

'But why should he knock you about?'

'Because I broke away, told them I wasn't going on.'

'Did Larry Paton arrange that – about Gallacher I mean?'

'No. Of course not. Larry's a friend. I did – what I did – for him. But I told you there are other people involved. It's funny about Gallacher in a way. There he is blundering about trying to prop up the whole dirty business while it's busting out all over the place. Someone told the police part of it.'

'Did you find out anything more about Nancy Douce?'

'I'm quite sure she is dead, but I don't know anything more about it than that. Don't think that Larry killed her! He's caught up in this business all right but he's no more capable of killing than you are. But Nancy Douce being dead – that's what it has all been about.'

'And Meg – my wife?'

'Nobody tried to kill her, Nick! It must be difficult to trust anything I say now, but I'm not lying any more. It was some sort of ghastly accident.'

Howard pointed back in the direction of the house where he'd been taken in the Mini. 'Some of the girls go on from those parties to another kind of party. Right?'

'More or less. Sometimes.'

'I thought so. I think that's what may have happened with Nancy. I'm going round to Park Place. Don't worry, I'm not going to try to hand out justice single-handed, but I want to ask Paton some questions.'

Jill shrugged. 'I don't think he'll be there. The police have been making some calls. No doubt Larry scarpered.'

'Well, I shall go there anyway. What about you?'

'I'm off too. I've got an aunt in Bodmin. She'll put me up for a while. I feel like getting away from everything. God, wouldn't it be marvellous if you could escape from yourself?'

Howard put his arm round her shoulders and signalled a passing taxi. 'You'll want to go to Paddington for Bodmin. He can drop me in Harley Street and then take you on.'

When they were seated in the taxi she leaned her head on his shoulder: she had a disconsolate expression.

'Come on, cheer up, Jill! I can't see that you've done anything very terrible. Well, nothing you can't live down. And you're so young. Time enough to make a completely different life. All clichés, I know, but absolutely true.'

'I suppose. It's a fact I'm looking forward a bit to Cornwall. It will be a breather. Shall sleep for twenty-four hours and then see how things look.'

'That's the idea. Spring's coming – a new year is opening up for you. Just forget Larry, and me too come to that. When you're young practically anything is possible.' He was not consciously handing her a bromide. The possibilities of youth did seem endless to him his own were much more limited, but the road before him did not dwindle away to nothing as it had before he met her.

They sat silently holding hands till the taxi came to the top of Harley Street. As he got out Jill said 'Thanks, Nick' and kissed him on the cheek. When the taxi moved off she used the limp tiger cub's paw to wave.

A man and a woman were standing with a collection of cases and cardboard boxes outside Park Place and for a moment

Howard wondered if he had caught Paton making his escape, though it seemed hardly likely that he would try it encumbered with so much luggage. When he approached them Howard saw it was the coloured couple who had served the refreshments at the masked party. The woman appeared slightly bewildered as she struggled with a case that wouldn't close properly, while the man's eyes looked as if he had just been involved in an argument and was cooling off. He had turned to go back into the house when Howard asked: 'Is Mr Larry Paton in there, do you know?'

The coloured man turned to look closely at Howard, and then replied in a dignified slow voice: 'This Park Place – Miss Dessart's house. Miss Jessica Dessart. Any questions about who-else in there you have to ask her. We don't work here no moah.' He nodded politely to Howard and went through the front door to pick up another carton in the hall.

'Is Miss Dessart in then?' Howard was thinking of Jessica Dessart's house in Grenada which had been vacated abruptly and left to moulder. What had Quincy said about that? Some scandal about a girl and an aphrodisiac. Was he going to find that an aged actress was at the bottom of Nancy's disappearance? He wanted to get more information from the man, who sounded as if he might be a Grenadian, and for a moment thought of saying that he'd seen Bellerêve as an introductory gambit, but the couple did not look as if they were in the mood for polite conversation.

The man pressed the gaping carton lid into place with care, apparently giving the question some thought. 'Yes, Miss Dessart is in. She here all right. But we finished, goin' right now. I don't work here so I can't announce you. But if you want to see her, why sure go ahead. She in the right mood for answerin' questions, telling everybody exac'ly what's what. You go on help yourself. This all our stuff now so that's that.' He looked round the hall once more, picked up the carton and walked out of the house.

When the door was slammed it seemed very cold in the house: there was a chill damp atmosphere of abandonment and slashed wrists. Howard knew this was largely in his mind – at a practical level it was probably a matter of the central heating system being switched off – but it added to his uneasiness at standing unasked in a strange house.

There was a sound of shuffling footsteps at the top of the stairs, and a querulous voice called out: 'Billy – is that you? Who is that down there?'

Howard walked up the stairs to where they curved back on themselves and saw a woman dressed in a dark grey trouser suit with gilt buttons and a black cardigan thrown over her shoulders. She looked too old to be Jessica Dessart and did not in the least resemble the photographs he had seen of her. Her face was haggard and much more lined than Edith Voysey's, and had an unhealthy leaden hue. But it was the desperate attempt to look young which made her appearance so pathetic. Her dry hair dyed brown was as artificial as a wig, and patches of green eye-shadow dashed on carelessly only focused attention on her moist eyes, which had a cringing expression like that of a beaten dog.

Howard was shocked and embarrassed. 'Miss Dessart? I'm Nicholas Howard. I'm sorry to trouble you. I think it may have been Billy who let me in – a coloured man. He's gone.'

'Has that dumb ox really left? Unbelievable. After all I've done for them! Oh well, they'll be back. And if not then to hell with them! Howard? Yes, I've heard of you. It ill behoves you to come here, whatever that may mean.'

'I came looking for Mr Larry Paton.'

'Then you're not the only one. There's a vast crowd of people out looking for Larry – he's never been so popular. And I haven't the faintest idea where he is. But if you've any other questions, just fire away. Tonight I'm in the mood for telling anybody anything they want to know. You see I've finished pimping for Larry and tidying up his messes. No more messes! That's my only consolation. Ask away – you behold in me a veritable oracle. I'll hand you out the truth all right. Whether you'll like it is another matter.' She tapped imperiously on the stair-rail with one waxy hand. Her breathing was slow and noticeable, with a faint whistling sound. She took a last puff at a cigarette and then dropped it on the carpet.

'I was going to ask Mr Paton about Nancy Douce.'

'Yes, I rather thought you were.' Her hands were shaking as she lit another cigarette. 'Poor little Nancy. I was very sorry about Nancy. It's quite simple what happened. It always is when something or someone gets smashed up. Smash! That's it – over in a second – and there's nothing can be done to put it right . . .' She looked vaguely about her as if she'd lost the point of what she was saying. 'I'm tired and that's the truth. Life, I've found Mr Howard, is so haphazard a business. A series of accidents with which one has to deal as best one can. Larry wanted Nancy. There! – that's the heart of the matter in three words. But Nancy did not want Larry and Larry wasn't the man to take no for an answer. So he laid a trap for her. First he found a clever medium, Madame Astrali, to get Nancy intrigued with the idea of contacting her father in the big beyond. The Madame is a fraud needless to say, but a very shrewd one, so that Nancy was never quite sure if she was just being strung along. Then from seances they moved on to a little magic, and from bogus magic to a fun trip with L S D. Larry fixed all that just for a chance to screw her! When I think of all the girls he's had! You can see the piquancy that's added when a girl really means no.' She made a clearing away motion with her free hand, to dissociate herself from the plot.

'Then one night, *not* here and I knew nothing about it, Nancy went to a party and was fed some more L S D. When the flight was over in the cold light of coming round she found she'd been in an orgy, used by Larry and several other – *men*.' She spat out the final word. 'What a crew of bastards! Anyway she was still out of control with the drug and she threw herself out of the window.'

Howard had sensed for some time that the denouement of Nancy's story might be like this, but to hear it authoritatively stated still left him feeling physically sick. There was a quotation from de Sade about all men wanting to be tyrants when they fornicated but it was one he rejected as being untrue – sadistic sex completely repelled him. He thought of the photograph of Nancy as a schoolgirl and shut his mind off from the raping scene.

'I've no doubt who master-minded that party – someone sicker than Larry. That midget monster Curtis Mahon. That freaky little toad. He should be . . .' She dropped her cigarette and ground it viciously into the carpet.

'Curtis Mahon?' Howard shook his head unbelievingly. 'But he sought me out. Why should he contact me knowing . . .'

Jessica Dessart waved this aside impatiently. 'Just because of your vague connection with Nancy. That tiny chess-playing psycho was thinking ten moves ahead as usual and decided that you, as a Knight or a Castle or something, would be blundering on the scene given enough time. So he decided to forestall any trouble by trying to tie you in. With some success surely?' she added coldly.

'Not enough to keep me quiet I assure you. What about my wife?'

Miss Dessart held her stomach, moving her hand in a prolonged comforting circular motion as if unaware of his presence. For a moment her eyes clouded with pain. When the spasm had passed she spoke in a dead voice: 'Your wife came here to see Larry shortly after Nancy had died. Larry tried to fob her off but she wasn't satisfied. Among other things she claimed to have some notes that Nancy had left in shorthand about one of the black magic sessions. So she left here threatening to bring in the police. Larry set off to talk her out of it, but she broke away in the street and he lost her in the crowd at Oxford Circus. He chased down on to the platform, startling her, and she fell. That's what happened there. You'll have to believe me, that was an accident. I know my Larry, by God I do, and he's no killer. Not that that's much comfort to you.'

The interview with Jessica Dessart had been like a series of blows and Howard felt numb as when at the end of boxing bouts he had kept on his feet only by an effort of will. Vaguely he was thinking of what he must do. First a phone call to the police, then one to Quincy who would be the best person to break the news to Mrs Douce.

'What happened to Nancy?'

'They had her dumped in the Thames – but – it's a bad joke like so much else – she got washed up somewhere. The police have her body. They have a lot of the story too. While the little evil genius was so sure you were the only possible source of trouble, some stray girl leaked something to Scotland Yard. A high-up cop has been playing it very close to his chest. But now he's pounced, and Mahon is safely locked up I'm glad to say.

Larry shot out of here hoping to get to France but I doubt if he made it ...' She smiled mirthlessly, as if nothing mattered much one way or the other. 'So that's that. Are you at all interested why I should tell you all this? No? Yes? It's very simple. The doctors have been cutting me open for the past year but now they've stopped. They've stopped jollying me along too. It's the big C. And I practically had to bribe someone to get the truth! What a world! – paying to hear your own death sentence! So you can see I've been set free from lies. And no more shady bits with Larry. I say to myself it's been a great relief throwing that off, but who am I trying to fool? What have I got instead? I tell you, it's like a bad dream when you can't wake up.'

Miss Dessart made an inconclusive gesture, then held her stomach again, pressing it as if she might subdue with a firm hand what was growing there. 'I'm so tired and yet I can't sleep. Bung full of junk, my eyes keep opening as if I'm still desperate to know what's going on. They said I should stay in the hospital but of course I was worried about Larry, and when I pressed them to let me leave they said okay. I knew then it didn't really make any difference either way.' She stared about with unseeing eyes. In her blank look Howard felt he glimpsed the image of the sand dollar god.

When she spoke again her tone was deliberately lighter, as if she were frightened she had gone on too long about her hopeless position. 'Stay with me a bit. Can you? I need someone to talk to. I'm tired of only seeing nurses. We could have a drink or some coffee perhaps.'

Howard nodded and covered with his own the parchment-pale hand that gripped the stair-rail. 'Sure. I'd like some coffee.' He had proved to be an indifferent investigator, but he knew he had learnt a lesson from this sad affair.

He went downstairs to look for the kitchen.